VAMPIRE LEGION

SHADOW ORDER: VAMPIRE BOOK FOUR

KRISTIN KOVA

Want an email when new books release? Join my mailing list: https://view.flodesk.com/pages/62716c5cec93244248595c00

Or follow me on Facebook: https://www.facebook.com/kristinkovaauthor/

Cover by Open World Cover Design

❈ Created with Vellum

A book capable of summoning and controlling all demons on Earth? *Adds to TBR*

London has gone to hell—literally. Lazarus, Keith, and I barely escaped Hell but now our city is crawling with demons who answer to one man. Lorn. The monster who killed me and made me a vampire.

The only way to stop him is to join him. The plan is simple: infiltrate Lorn's cabal of twisted vampires, and take them down from the inside. But my new demon magic is hungry, and the more I use it, the more it wants to destroy.

With the dark codex back in my hands, I have unlimited power at my fingertips. Enough to wipe Lorn off the face of the map. Or to become just like him.

This is one book I should have left on the shelf.

KRISTIN KOVA

VAMPIRE LEGION

THE SHADOW ORDER: VAMPIRE 4

This book is for the quiet, bookish people always off on adventures inside their own heads but too anxious to have real life adventures.

ONE

I stared up at the black and white Tudor pub and wondered if I'd make it out of the building alive. I hesitated on the pavement, scuffing my boots against the worn stone long enough that a black cab ploughed through a puddle gathered in a crater between cobbles, splashing my legs with dirty brown water. The shriek I let out made me sound almost human, almost normal, and for a moment I felt like the old Karina. But the old Karina would have fled to somewhere safe instead of standing outside a pub that housed the worst and darkest of vampire kind.

Hurt and rejection had fuelled my angry dash across the city, but now I was here, now I'd found *him,* all my courage fled. I remembered being thrown across the Witching Library and left to die in a broken heap, remembered the smooth, slimy drawl of his voice as he compelled me.

"You're not that broken mortal anymore," I whispered, so low even the supernatural ears within wouldn't hear my pep talk. "You're stronger than all of them."

And I was. With my inferno, with demon magic surging through me, forging my vampire body into something stronger, something *better,* I knew I could handle this. I could handle anything. No one could hurt me now.

But I still hesitated long enough to wring the ditch water from my jeans, glancing furtively around the dingy little backstreet not too far from the historic Borough Market. I'd walked through it to get here, the usually bustling market stalls eerily still, the old roads around it lit by yellow streetlights and the errant ray of silvered moonlight. Just weeks ago, I would have been nervous to be alone in the city at night, but the only thing making me nervous now was the thought of my grandsire. I was a match for him now, or maybe I would even disintegrate him with a single burst of fire, but fear had burrowed deep and wouldn't listen to logic.

"He's one man," I muttered, and picked up my feet, my nose wrinkling at the way wet fabric clung to my legs.

This was undoubtedly a bad idea, but I pushed open the door to the pub and walked inside.

Eight hours before

Lorn is right. The words I'd said replayed in my head in an annoying loop, and I grew more irate with every pass as I trudged into the kitchen of the house on the banks of the Thames. Lazarus followed me like a shadow. He refused to let me out of his sight since I engulfed every Hell portal on Earth in hot, destructive fire. The memory brought a smile to my face, and a flicker of flames danced down my fingers. It felt good to burn away my fear, to finally be freed of the paralysing anxiety I'd had since I became a vampire against my will. No, since before that. Maybe for the first time ever, I didn't have panic and stress holding me back; I was liberated, and powerful. And hungry.

My throat was as dry as sandpaper and getting dryer with every hour, a rawness rasping up to my tongue. I needed to feed, had probably burned through too much energy closing the portals, locking all the demons in Hell. But it was worth it. Nothing like what Invequius did to us would ever happen again. He was dead and gone, and they were *all* trapped. We were safe. I never had to be afraid again.

I made a beeline for the crisscross shelving on the far wall and pulled out a bottle of red wine from a selection worth thousands.

"Can I trust you with a corkscrew?" Lazarus remarked, leaning against the counter to watch me, the room dark around us now the sun had set, moonlight and my enhanced sight enough to make out the trepidation in his eyes.

I sighed. "I thought the issue was my magic, but now I'm going to use a corkscrew as a weapon?"

He was being dramatic. Sure, I was full of power and the fire was dangerous, but I felt *good*. I was in control.

Humans are too weak, too breakable to rule. We should be leading the world.

I winced as my own voice replayed. I didn't entirely regret the words; one drop of the fire inside my body was enough to burn a human to a crisp. They *were* too break-able, too vulnerable. It was plain stupid that there were creatures as dangerous and powerful as us in the world, and *we* were the ones hiding in the shadows, crawling out of sight. We should at least have equal claim to the world.

Lazarus watched me warily, the expression on his pale, aquiline face almost tired as I poured two glasses and handed one to him. He accepted it with a sigh, sipping the rich liquid.

"This power—" he began.

"*My* power," I corrected. "It's a part of me."

His dark red eyes were heavy on me. The disappoint-ment in them hit me like a knife to the chest. "It's burning you up inside and you can't even feel it. Mum said you need to purge it from your system, find a way to safely remove it from you before it can do any more damage."

I blinked, taking a slow sip of wine, the rich fruit exploding on my taste buds. Not as good as blood, but enough. For now. "Any *more* damage," I repeated, clinking my claws against the glass. They'd yet to recede, and so had my horns and my wings. I didn't ask if my eyes were still black.

Rus's stare was deep with sadness, his face drawn. "Karina, you're acting... different."

At that, a disbelieving laugh puffed from me. I set down the glass, my emotions spiky, memories trying to form in my head. I didn't let them. "Different?" I echoed.

"Rus, for the first time in my life I'm not scared of anything. I'm happy, *we* can be happy. There are no demons to threaten us, no open portals, and we can finally deal with Lorn now that he has no demon army coming to his rescue. We can be *happy*, Rus," I repeated, resting my hands on his chest.

"This demon magic—" My stomach plummeted when he pulled away, just an inch but enough to make it clear he was rejecting me. A furrow knotted my brow, hurt twisting my heart. I'd just lost a woman I loved more than anyone else in the world, and now Rus was pulling away because I'd unlocked a well of power? Because I'd finally found my inner strength? Because I wasn't the scared, shaking girl he'd thrown in the cell downstairs?

My eyes burned, but I wouldn't cry. I sank deeper into my flames, letting them chase away the chill of Rus's rejection. Everything had been good between us, incredible actually. Seeing the wariness and disappointment in his eyes hit even harder because our relationship was so new.

"Fine," I said before he could continue, a truth settling into my bones. He didn't want this new, improved version of me. He would never understand me now I was powerful and strong and unafraid. I looked at him and found him watching me sadly, and I wondered if he'd realised what I had.

I didn't belong here anymore.

TWO

Deep down, I knew I was being rash and letting hurt cloud my judgement, but the inferno encouraged me. It told me I was *right* to be hurt, that my mate had rejected me, that he would never accept me now I'd changed.

Lazarus was distracted, his eyes tight with stress, so it was easier to slip away than it should have been. When the phone rang, bringing news of the council's decision, I slipped into the hallway. The growling sigh Lazarus released was enough to tell me they were still stalling. Sorry, *deliberating*. The council had deliberated for so long that I'd already closed the portals that were a threat to everyone on Earth. They'd probably still be in discussions when the portals reopened again whenever someone else thirsted for power. The thought of them opening again, the possibility of getting thrown back in Hell made me angry.

No, it made me *furious*.

Heat bubbled beneath my skin, my skin turning pink

as I hurried soundlessly down the hallway, a pang in my chest at the thought of not seeing it for a while. But I'd be back. When Rus had some time to come to terms with my new power, when he'd accepted me for me, and when Lorn was dead, I'd come back. This was more my home now than the house I shared with Mum and Aunt Jubilee.

I physically flinched. *Don't think about Jubilee.*

The sharp scent of the Thames smacked me in the face when I gently closed the front door behind myself, but I broke into a run before the chill air could offer any comfort. I needed to run far and fast before Lazarus caught up to me. Because he would—he'd search for me, and he wouldn't stop until he found me. The mate bond would see to that, I presumed. *But* if I was fast enough, I could find Lorn before Lazarus tracked me down.

Lorn deserved to die. He was the reason Jubilee was dead, the whole reason Invequius was able to use her to control me in the first place. The reason Invequius even knew I existed. I remembered that first day in the angel temple, remembered the sickly feeling of the demon's attention, the way my skin crawled.

My anger flashed hotter, thick steam curling off my arms now, thick and visible against the cold night air as I ran, pushing myself as fast as my body would allow.

London flew past as I tugged my hood over my horns and sprinted along familiar pathways, following the Thames past the Globe, past the Witching Library, and further, until the shape of the council building rose above me. Part of me wanted to drag my feet and enter the library, to find some solace and comfort among the stacks of weathered paper and dyed leather, but the last time I was there, Lazarus and I were hunted. It didn't offer the same comfort anymore. Just another thing I'd lost since Keaton scratched me and Lorn threw me to my death.

I should have died that day; I shouldn't even have been here. A fluke, a coincidence—that's what saved me. If I had died crushed beneath shelves and broken books, would Jubilee have survived?

"Don't think of that now," I muttered, not even out of breath after the flight across the city. Even if I'd felt the cold against my skin, the inferno would have kept me warm, flames licking higher. As much as I told myself not to think about it, I couldn't help it. We'd been happy, Jubilee, Mum, and I. We'd been safe and perfectly content, no demons in our lives, no forced trips to Hell, no sacrifices, no screaming hordes or scheming vampires.

Lorn took that from me. I'd give all this power up to have my aunt back.

You're the best niece anyone could ask for. And as much my daughter as you are my sister's.

A chink formed in my rage, but I brought Lorn's face to the front of my mind and made my way up the formidable stone steps and into the council building. Unlike the last time I was here, I barely saw any of it. Was that really only hours ago? I felt like a whole different person as I strode through the pale stone atrium, far fewer people streaming around me than before but still enough that I went unnoticed by the reception staff.

I didn't know how to use the sire bond, but my demon magic did. A tiny ripple went through my belly but the unease was quickly swallowed by the pit of lava that expanded with every breath. I followed the tug in my gut down a long, high-ceilinged corridor lined with gold marble columns, my back straight and chin up, expression determined like I belonged here and had a task to do. No one looked at me like I was out of place, even with the horns and wings, even as I took two right turns and ended up at a staircase leading *up*—not down as I expected. The gleaming marble and gold details ended here, giving way to bare stone lit by a single bare bulb swinging overhead, a tiny window at the landing above me offering another square of light.

I didn't question the inferno's guidance. It had never led me wrong before; because of it, I was alive and all the portals were slammed shut. Because of the inferno, I was safe. And Rus wanted me to give up that safety?

I tucked my wings tight and ascended the stairs, sure that if I'd been mortal a chill would have settled into my bones. It was the sort of staircase that led to a gothic lair, where someone's wife would be shoved in the attic. Fitting for a vampire, though I'd much rather be curled up in the library at home with the fire crackling comfortingly, Keith snoring on the arm of the chair, and a book open on my lap.

Soon, I promised myself, and ignored all the obstacles between me and that cosy scene. It would have been a better fantasy if Rus was there with me, but even my imagination was mad at him. How dare he tell me something was wrong? How dare he act like this fire thrumming inside me hadn't saved his mother and gotten us all out of Hell?

I reached the landing and forged on, taking the steps cautiously even if I wanted to sprint up them at full speed. I needed to measure my steps, keep my ears pricked, and not look suspicious. With all the power I had now, I doubted anyone would be strong enough to throw me out of the council building, but I'd rather not risk it.

My fire seemed to bank like it was disappointed it wouldn't be unleashed.

These people aren't our enemies, I reminded it, reminded myself. Killing them served no purpose. So, I kept scaling the stairs on light feet, ignoring the tiny voice in my head that screamed I had no plan and everything was going to go wrong. I'd be fine. I was deadly now.

At the top of another flight of stairs, a grey stone hallway spread out in two ways on either side of me, the scent of unwashed bodies, overcooked food, industrial cleaning fluids, and piss combining to make me gag. I cut off my air so I didn't have to smell it, but it was stuffed up my nose now, curdling my stomach with a visceral sickness. I'd never been happier that I didn't need to breathe.

Invequious laughed, the sound rumbling around me, raising the hairs on the back of my neck and making it impossible to breathe.

"I'm not afraid of you anymore," I hissed under my breath, scanning the hallway like there'd be a clue to where my quarry was. I listened to the thrashing fire inside me, trying to shut out how badly it wanted to come out and burn down this whole building. I turned right.

Finally, Invequius breathed, his voice inside my head. I've been dying to find out what lives inside this stubborn mind of yours. Oh, so much suffering, so much pain.

"Shut up," I snarled at my own subconscious, the memories unwelcome. I was *free*. I wasn't trapped there with him controlling me anymore. He was dead; Keith ate him. There was no trace left. I was free.

Won't you be relieved to be free?

I needed to get his voice out of my head *now*. Every time his voice slid through my memories, the fire roared a little louder, climbed a little higher, until my skin heated, little curls of steam rising from me. I walked faster, the sound of my rough footsteps echoing off the stone all around me, grounding me in the present. He wasn't here. He was never coming back.

But that didn't unlock the band around my chest and didn't stop the shiver down my spine as I crossed the empty corridor. Shouldn't there have been a guard here to keep the prisoners inside? Had my fire had even brought me to the right place?

My path ended at a left turn, and I was so distracted by memories of Invequius that I forgot to scout the corner before I followed it. A rough hand locked around my forearm, and I took a forceful gasp, my eyes watering at the sudden onslaught a rancid smell made on my senses.

Panic struck so severely that I forgot I was a vampire and frantically pulled at the grip, wide eyes snapping up to stare at the broad-shouldered, grey-skinned man looming over me. He was physically intimidating, with wings that blotted out the tiny bit of light coming from a window behind him, and his rough-hewn features were stern with warning. Gargoyle.

Fear made my skin tingle, a shiver poised on the back of my neck.

"No visitors authorised today," he barked in a voice like boulders grating. I'd worked with a gargoyle at the library; he'd been sweet and kind with a lilting voice and an easy smile. This man was nothing like that.

When he tossed me away and released his grip on my arm, as if his intimidation would send me scurrying away, I remembered myself. I cut off breathing and straightened my spine, lifting my chin.

"Where is Keaton?"

The words came out low and sonorous, coercive. I'd never spoken this way before, but I remembered all the times Rus had compelled me and a thrill went through my chest. Was I finally strong enough to do it, too? And on a gargoyle no less.

One glance at his eyes killed that dream and I jerked back just as he lunged for me.

"I said," he grated out, "no visitors today."

His scowl and the way he kept *grabbing* me had anger burning through my chest, and I cocked my chin higher, not fighting the rush and flow of the inferno this time. I'd rather not hurt staff members, but this gargoyle was in my way.

"One chance," I warned, my eyes narrowed on the man as he widened his stance, clearly blocking access to the heavy wooden door behind him. It wasn't another hallway at all, but an entrance. I'd put blood and money on that door leading to the cells. I'd never even known there were prisoners held up here; all the rumours spoke about a dungeon belowground. I had the feeling I'd stumbled upon a high-security secret I was never meant to know.

"One chance," the gargoyle repeated in a scoff. "What are you going to do? Bite me? I'm made of stone."

I tilted my head, considering him. He was probably very good at his job, and I bet he scared off most people trying to enter this place. But I wasn't most people. I was forcibly turned into a vampire, taunted by a demon, dragged into Hell, and reforged there into something new. Bane—that was what I was now. Not quite vampire, not entirely demon, nothing remotely close to human.

It was easy to grasp the power. Too easy.

"Where is Keaton?" I repeated my question, sinking into the inferno like I'd sink into a hot bath, tension massaged from my tight muscles, the band around my chest easing.

You know, he mused, I planned to snuff you out the second I claimed this body, but I think I'll leave you conscious. It'll be fun to hear you struggle.

He couldn't hurt me now. Invequius was dead. Even if he wasn't, I knew with the flames rising higher inside me, making crimson hair dance around my shoulders, turning my skin smooth and pink, I could kill him. It would take little effort. Less to remove this stone obstacle in my way.

The gargoyle probably had a family waiting for him to return at the end of the day. Librarian Karina would have cared about that. Vampire Karina would have faltered. But Bane Karina? I lifted a hand and fire poured over the guard from his boots to his knees, climbing up thighs as wide as tree trunks, over his stomach and chest, until it ringed his throat. It happened so fast he couldn't scream, could only widen his eyes before those too were engulfed.

"Fangs can't do much to stone," I said, kneeling beside

the pile of blackened rocks on the floor in front of me, life-less and degraded. "But even stone is susceptible to fire."

I rose in a swift motion. If I'd had a heart, it would have quickened as I faced the door. "Should have taken the one chance I gave you to run," I told the gargoyle and stepped over the charred remains, wrapping my fingers around the cool door handle.

I expected resistance, but it opened willingly, almost welcoming me into the dark, unsettling row of cells beyond it.

With a smile of victory, I stepped inside and let the door fall shut.

THREE

There were three occupants of this delightful prison, so it was easy to find Keaton. He was slumped in the corner formed by two grey, pockmarked walls, one of which held a loop of thick, vampire-grade metal where the chains at his wrist had been pinned to. A bucket sat across the small cell from him, its contents making me relieved I'd stopped breathing on the other side of the heavy door.

The other two men didn't bother to look up at the sound of my intentional footsteps, my boots scuffing the smooth stone tiles underfoot, but Keaton slid his eyes in my direction. They were bleak eyes full of suffering. My lips stretched into a smile.

"This is a lovely sight," I told him, toeing the bars between us. "I always dreamed of you rotting to death somewhere. Tell me, are they starving you?"

"Fuck you," he spat, turning away from me like the wall was a more riveting conversation partner.

I toed the solid iron bars at the front of his cell with

my boot, soaking in the sight of his suffering. I was a vampire because of him. My aunt was gone because of him. Keaton deserved everything he got.

"What's with the wings?" he asked, his upper lip curling back like he had any right to judge someone's appearance. His hair was slicked to his skull by grease and (hopefully) other gross fluids, and the black button-up shirt and jeans he wore were similarly grimy, like he'd been wearing them for days in this place. With any luck, he'd still be in them months later. He was going to rot in this place for a nice, long time. I wouldn't kill him; that was too easy. Too merciful. Why would I give mercy to a monster like him?

Like you, a tiny voice countered, but it was drowned out by my rage and my satisfaction at seeing Keaton so broken.

"Where is Lorn?" I demanded, not wasting time on small talk.

Keaton laughed, a hoarse, twisted thing, and turned back to the wall. "You think he tells me anything?"

"I think you were close enough to know where he's hiding. Tell me."

"He cut me out, you stupid girl—"

A rush of inferno poured through my chest. I spat through the bars of the cell and smirked when tiny flames landed on my sire, making him hiss in panic as he frantically slapped the embers out.

"What the hell *are* you?" he asked, watching me with new horror, new *fear*. Oh, that felt good. I wanted him to be afraid of me.

"I am what you made me, Keaton. So I'll ask again—

and this time, keep in mind that I can burn you alive —*where is Lorn?*"

"I don't know."

When I lifted my hand, crimson flames sparking at my fingertips, he rushed to add, "But I know where you can find someone who *will* know. The rest of Lorn's cabal are... different. Vampires but fucking creepy. Like you."

"Aw, that hurts my feelings."

He must have meant the other bondlings Vala warned Rus about. Vampires who'd been possessed with a demon bond forced on them, like Invequius forced on me. The portals only locked Hell; there could be hundreds of demons already here. Closing the portals might not have stopped Lorn at all.

"If I tell you where to find one of them," Keaton said warily, not bothering to get up from his spot in the corner. Maybe he couldn't; he was chained to the wall after all. "You'll leave me alone?"

"You'll never see me again," I agreed. If I never saw him as long as I lived, it would still be too soon. Not that I was technically living.

"One of them is called Birdie. She lives above a Thai restaurant in Holborn, but that's all I know. If you find her, she'll lead you to Lorn. Now leave me the fuck alone."

"With pleasure," I said, taking one last look at him, at his bucket of filth, at his rancid conditions.

I walked away with a smirk.

FOUR

There were only a few Thai restaurants near Holborn; I started with the first hit on Google. I had to slip someone's phone from their pocket in order to use the internet, since I left mine at home like an idiot, but needs must. And Lorn *needed* to pay.

I curled my hands into fists to hide the fire spitting from my fingers at the thought of that bastard. Keaton was bad enough, had committed enough crimes, but Lorn took sick enjoyment in the pain he delivered. I remembered every smile, every silken word, every *laugh,* and it became harder to contain my fire. I exhaled a cloud of crimson, lucky there were only a few people out on the streets at this time of night. With my inferno raging and my fury even hotter, I wasn't sure how I'd handle a human witnessing me losing control. Vauxhall Bridge came back to me with enough clarity to make me flinch, and the remembered taste of blood filled my mouth. My thirst scraped its way up my throat, reminding me I didn't feed earlier. Maybe I'd drain Lorn dry before I murdered him. There was a sort of poetic justice in that.

I slipped down a side street before my thirst could convince me to draw a deep breath and scent the nearest warm, pumping vein. The door to the flat above the Thai restaurant was easy enough to find, and my strength made ramming the door in easy. If this flat didn't belong to Birdie, I'd feel a little bad for the damage, but at least I wasn't planning to rob the place.

I crept silently up the tall flight of stairs ahead of me, the steps worn in the middle by high traffic over many years, white paint chipped off to reveal wood beneath. I placed my feet in each of those worn spots, keeping my attention fixed on the landing above, where a single door marked the apartment. That made it easier than being faced with two or more flats. Either this was Birdie's home and I'd found my place, or I'd know quickly this was a bust and I could find the next Thai restaurant.

I glanced down at the claws on my fingers, my lips tilting up at the corners as I approached the door. Who needed lockpicks when you had claws?

It took three attempts but the soft snick of the lock turning was immensely satisfying. My blood roared with the victory of it. Or maybe that was just the inferno dancing in excitement at the thought of a fight. With any luck, Birdie would tell me what I wanted to know without an altercation, but my fire was ready for either eventuality.

The door swung open on a butter-yellow room decorated depressingly with sparse furniture, only an armchair set up in front of a television propped on a stack of books.

In the corner, a small kitchen crouched by the window. The vibrant paint on the walls was the only attempt at making the place homely, the rest of it bare, and a longing for home hit me so suddenly and fiercely that I sucked in a breath.

Scents triggered my sense of taste. Bagged blood, mould, lemon disinfectant, and the floral brightness of perfume. It wasn't a combination I was expecting, and it got my hackles up. A vampire definitely lived here. I tucked my dark wings tighter to my back and peered around the room, all my senses heightened, my fingertips alive with fire.

I waited for any sign of movement, my ears pricked for a shift of weight, a single exhale, a gasp of surprise. When there was nothing, I stepped inside the apartment and headed for the only other door, presumably leading to a bedroom. Whoever lived here, they clearly weren't home, so I wasted no time rummaging through their stuff, searching for any connection to Lorn. I found a stash of blood bags in a temperature-controlled box, and an old book on vampirism, but otherwise nothing.

I was just sliding out another drawer in the bedroom when an intentional shift of feet on floorboards made me freeze.

"Come out, little prey, and I might kill you quickly," a sultry female voice called from the entrance.

Fear ought to have made me cold but it was red-hot fury that blazed through me, building until my palms covered in deep blue flame. It burned hot enough to ruffle my hair as I held them in front of myself and stepped out of the room.

"Who are you calling prey?" I demanded, the demon magic that lived inside me absolutely *livid*.

The woman who'd spoken was tall and curvaceous with deep caramel skin, beautiful features, and luxurious brunette hair that cascaded in glossy waves to her waist. She looked like she'd walked out of a shampoo ad. I was going to rip the pretty hair from her head. *Prey. Me?*

My fire flashed hotter, *writhing* under my skin.

"Who are *you* to intrude in my home?" she retorted, flowing a step closer, definitely a vampire by the way she moved. I made sure to match her step but with an awkward gait, hoping she'd think I was mortal if I kept my hood up and my wings mostly behind me. If she was going to think I was *prey* I might as well play on that misconception.

"I'm looking for someone called Birdie."

She tilted her head in a rapid swoop, that glossy hair falling over her shoulder. "Are you now? Well, you've found her. Who sent you to me?"

She eyed me like I was dinner a friend had sent via JustEat. *That* was my last straw. I was no one's prey and no one's damn food. I was a Bane. The Bane of all demons, I decided, and all those who would help them invade London.

I was across the room in a blink, wrapping hands of flame around her throat. Birdie was ready for me, grabbing a fistful of my hair, but she didn't step back or try to dislodge my grip even as her flesh bubbled under my fiery hands. The flicker of excitement in her eyes told me she would enjoy this fight.

"Where is Lorn?"

Birdie's laugh bounced around the room, grating my patience to a thin filament. "That old bastard? Haven't seen him in months. Why would you want to find him?"

I dug my claws into her skin, the scent of rich, honeyed blood filling the air. Oh, she was definitely enjoying this and it was right there in her sweet-smelling blood. My mouth filled with saliva; I had to swallow before I could speak.

"I know you're one of his pet bondlings." I let a smile fill my face and wondered if there were flames dancing in my eyes. "So am I. I got a little lost, but I want to find my way back to him."

"You're a fool," Birdie said with a dismissive snort. "You're better off far from him."

"Alright," I sighed and punched my claws deeper into her throat, so she knew I wasn't messing around. "I'll take that under advisement. But I still need to know where to find him."

A knee slammed up between my legs, hitting with vampire strength and a new sense of self-preservation. My eyes filled with blood tears, my nostrils flaring at the pain, but I held on with a snarl, grinding my claws into her spinal cord.

"You're fucking crazy," she said, rasping around my claws in her throat.

I snapped my wings out and watched her face pale, her ruby eyes widening. But she slammed a fist into my ribs with enough force that I felt one crumple, and she struggled against my grip with superior vampire speed and strength. Luckily, my inferno roared hotter and higher, trickling down her body in a scorched coil from her throat to her shoulders and all the way down her arms.

"Stop. Fuck. I'll tell you where he is." Birdie's next hit knocked all the wind from me, and my grip on her throat fumbled, but my fire was the greater threat than my claws. "What the fuck are you?" she asked in ragged horror.

"I'm just like you," I replied, unable to keep the smile off my face. It felt good to let my power out, to stop holding it back even if only for a few minutes. No pretending I was still the scared seer forcibly turned by two bastard vampires.

I was wicked and strong and I loved it.

"I'm nothing like you," Birdie breathed, fighting harder, hitting me with another hit to my rib, right over the fracture. I grunted, my vision blurring for a split second.

"Descend into Hell," I laughed, a little twisted, "and you'll see. You're exactly like me. Now where the fuck is Lorn?"

I snarled through gritted teeth, the pain growing when I was forced to take a breath to speak. The scent of blood had thickened, the sweetness enough to make my mouth flood with saliva. My pain made it even more tempting. Hot, fresh blood pouring from her throat. Inviting. Dangerously good.

"He and his little gang live above a pub in Chelsea. The Hobgoblin. That's all I can tell you; I left those psychos months ago when I found out they want to subjugate humans."

She eyed me, seemingly realising I might want the same thing. I sighed. It wasn't like I wanted humans collared in cages or even with their rights stripped, but we deserved to come out of the darkness and into the light with equal power. We had more magic, more strength, more longevity than all of them; it was time we were truly equals. Lorn was right about that much.

"The Hobgoblin," I repeated. "Thank you."

The little flutter of her eyes suggested relief when I removed one of my hands from her neck. I assumed the relief died in the next second when I struck, burying my fangs in her throat and gulping down her blood, but I couldn't see her face. My eyes were too busy sliding shut at the glorious sweetness of her blood, my thirst slaked as my belly filled with rich life giving fluid. She fought bravely, struggling against me, getting a few good hits before she weakened.

When Birdie slumped, weak against my front, I drew my fangs out and licked the last few drops of blood from my fangs. Then I snapped her neck and tore her heart from her chest.

I couldn't risk Lorn using her—and the demon she'd bonded to—for more power. And every blow to him made me and my infernal fire mutually happy.

FIVE

This was undoubtedly a bad idea. Lorn was much older than me, and far more cunning. His plan had fallen through because I closed the portals, but as I pushed open the heavy door to the Hobgoblin I heard his laughter roll down the carpeted stairs behind the bar. And again I wondered if we'd stopped his play for power at all. The taproom was empty of customers, not a single person downstairs. No one came to investigate the creak of the door, as if they were used to people coming and going.

I approached the bar, pushing up the divider, and assessed the wine on offer, pouring myself a glass of cabernet while I listened to the voices coming from upstairs. Two men and a woman were talking about the gates to Hell being sealed. My whole body stiffened at the sound of Lorn's silky voice.

"It changes nothing," he cut in, soothing an argument about to begin. "We don't need more. We have all the demons we need already here."

I finished the last of my glass, wiped the wine and blood from my face, and slipped into the short hallway behind the bar, heading up the stairs as soundlessly as I'd entered Birdie's flat.

"Speaking of everyone you need," I cut in, leaning against the doorway at the top of the stairs. I swept a quick glance over a room decorated in rich crimson patterns and jewel toned furniture. There were three people, like I suspected, one female and short with a shock of cerise hair, one male with deep umber skin and an imposing height, and Lorn, looking as elegant and smug and superior as ever. His sleek hair was tied back from his face, his clothes likely designer.

"Whatever is happening here, I want in."

They all spun like they'd been jolted, and that was my first clue that my senses might be superior to theirs thanks to my Bane form. The other two had to be bondlings like me, maybe even with demons living inside them, but they'd never had wings and horns and claws forced out of them by the sheer desperate survival of being in Hell. Like me but not, exactly like Birdie.

"You shouldn't leave your front door open," I told Lorn casually, meeting his tight gaze when he stared at me. "Just about anyone could walk in."

"You want in," he repeated in a scoff, watching me carefully, measuring me, wondering just how I got so close to them without anyone noticing. "Lazarus's goody two-shoes little pet? You seriously expect me to believe that?"

I tilted my head, watching him as he watched me. I saw him mark the horns coming from my head when I removed my hood, and the claws vicious at the ends of my fingers, the wings visible over my shoulders, a hooked talon at each apex.

"Who says I'm good?" I took a step into the room, a little thrilled at the way they reacted. The pink-haired woman rose from the armchair where she'd been sitting in front of the window, the other man edging closer, recognising me as a threat. *See, Birdie, that's how you react to someone like me.* Prey. The word still irritated me, making my skin hot from within.

The real prey was right in front of me, watching me with amusement and a perpetual smugness that made me want to punch him. Glossy hair, a too-perfect face, pearly teeth. I would knock those teeth out when I killed him. But I needed to know what he meant by *the demons already here.* Killing him would be satisfying, but not until my home was purged of all demons.

"Who is this?" the pink-haired vampire asked, watching me warily but with a brittle edge, like she was threatened by me. Aw, were she and Lorn together? How cute.

Lorn didn't answer her, didn't take his gleaming eyes off me. "You seriously want me to believe you've had such a change of heart? I seem to remember you being disgusted and angry before."

"Before this?" I snapped my wings out, sending ornaments and photo frames crashing off a chest of drawers beside me, gouging a nice line in the wall to my right. "Yeah. I *was* disgusted. Now?" I advanced a step, holding his stare. "I went through Hell. I saw true evil there, true darkness, and I *became* the darkness. You started this by putting me on Invequius's radar. He's dead by the way."

"She's telling the truth," the tall, black man murmured, as if he was a lie detector in vampire form. Or maybe it was the demon speaking through him?

"Always truthful, aren't you, Karina?" Lorn asked, his voice lower, halfway between a taunt and a purr. "What's to stop you running right to my *sire* with everything you learn here?" He said the word sire like a curse.

I laughed—and *laughed*, letting the bitter hurt of Rus's rejection fill the room in a manic cackle. "Lazarus and I are done. He loved sweet, meek little Karina, and she died in Hell."

The bondling woman was edging closer; I saw her in my periphery and let her come. Did she know she was a mouse creeping up on a lion?

"This is all very convenient," Lorn remarked, an eyebrow raised when I snapped my wings in, the movement sudden enough that the man whose name I didn't know jumped. I smiled. "What's more realistic is that you came here to spy on us."

Pink blurred in the edge of my vision. I lashed my hand out and enjoyed the moment of shocked, frozen silence when my fingers thrust through skin and muscle and bone, shattering her ribcage so I could pull out her heart. She hit the floor with a solid thud, not even a cry of pain leaving her.

I gave Lorn a little smile, warm blood rolling down my wrist, dripping to the floor. I was aware I'd crossed a moral line, that something had shifted in my soul and psyche, but that didn't stop me lifting my hand so I could lick the line of her blood from my hand.

"Waste not, want not. Any more questions?" I asked, holding eye contact.

There was a bright flare of excitement in Lorn's eyes, his smile a little sharper. "I think that will be all. Bourne, get the woman a drink."

And just like that, I was in.

SIX

The red lines left on my skin had faded in the hours since we left Hell, but I could see the faint scars they'd left. I massaged them as I lounged on the bed in my new box room above the Hobgoblin, left to my own devices for the first time in hours. I'd weathered the interrogation Lorn, Bourne, and three other members of his little gang unleashed on me. The other names didn't rhyme, sadly. I'd been amused by the Lorn, Bourne situation for a few minutes. They didn't exactly trust me, but they'd stopped looking at me suspiciously now. And I'd clearly won them over enough because I would tag along when they left in a few hours, at three a.m.

I had a feeling it was more a test or initiation than anything, but I'd be fine. I'd gotten this far, and answers were so close I could taste them. All I needed to do was spend enough time with this gang of vampires, uncover their demonic plot, ruin everything they had planned, and then kill them. Then I'd be safe, with no demons left to possess me, to cage me in my body, to threaten the ones I loved ever again. I'd never lose anyone else.

My mind went over and over how I'd kill Lorn, how I'd eliminate each of his minions, and I was so deep in the fantasies that I didn't realise I was sucking the last remnants of the pink-haired vampire's blood from my fingers. I didn't eat her heart, I wasn't that crazy, but I couldn't deny that I'd been tempted to. Bourne's calm, sage mask had shattered for a moment when I made to throw the organ in the bin; he'd leapt across the room with a hiss and snatched it from my hand, devouring it in four bites. I wasn't sure if that was normal Bourne behaviour or if the demon bond had shown its face then. I wasn't sure how many were possessed the way Invequius had threatened to do to me.

I couldn't let my guard down with any of the bondlings. I might have my inferno and enough magic to take out all of them, but anyone could sneak up on my back and render all that power useless.

At ten to three, I hauled myself off the bed, surprised at how comfortable it was, and scanned the street below through the small window beside the bed. It was raining heavily, the street soaked through. No demon army lying in wait. No bondlings hovering around, either. Had I worried for nothing, and Lorn's cabal was made up of four people? No wonder he'd allowed me to stay.

Although, I *had* ripped the heart from a woman's chest. That was pretty convincing.

Satisfied no ambush was waiting—outside, at least—I cracked the door open and made my way downstairs to where voices overlapped in the taproom. Bourne was leaning against the bar when I took the final step, bulging brown arms crossed over his chest and exposed by the black vest he wore with leather trousers. Typical vampire attire. At the other end of the vampire spectrum, Lorn sat like an imperious prince in his designer suit and shiny shoes, with his perfect hair and polished teeth.

Their little group was rounded out by three others. Griffin, a mixed race man in his thirties—although appearances could be deceiving—with smooth brown skin, delicate features, and short twists of black hair. He eschewed both vampire styles with a sheer white blouse over jeans. He also gave me a fluttering little wave of his fingers when he spotted me, delight in his ruby eyes. He hadn't liked the pink-haired woman much, I'd learned.

"Darling Karina," he purred, holding out a hand for mine as I walked around the bar. I ignored it. "You look ravishing."

"Thanks," I said dryly, watching the two other bondlings. They had the exact same features—sharp chin, heart-shaped face, a straight nose, and skin so pale it had to have been fair even before they transitioned. They must have been twins but where one had long white hair, the other had hair the colour of dried blood. Same narrow, sultry eyes. Same smirking mouth. Same height, same silhouette, even the same dark red lipstick and black lace gown. Ember and Aspen.

I looked at Lorn, the ringleader of this little ground, and wondered again if there were more minions, more bondlings, or if this was *it*. "Where are we going?"

Lorn gave me a slow once over, his small eyes critical of what he found. Asshole. "Westminster," he answered, picking up a brown leather satchel from the table and rising to his feet.

He strode out the door with no further explanation. With a sigh, ignoring the rest of the group, I followed.

I COULD FEEL THE TWINS' eyes bearing holes in the back of my head, but I kept my chin high as we ran at vampire speed across London, stopping only when we were inside the gates around the Houses of Parliament. I couldn't keep the confusion off my face; what were we doing here?

I'd expected a pit in the ground or a gathering of demon soldiers or even a prince of Hell waiting for us. I hadn't expected Big Ben to tower above us, the slow chug of traffic hissing on the rain-slick road that flowed across Westminster Bridge to Waterloo. Even at night, there were police officers guarding the entrances to the vast building, but without a spoken order the twins sped towards them, a quick word dropping the officers to the ground in a heap as the women ran to the next entrance, and around the side, presumably to another.

"Why the Houses of Parliament?" I asked, keeping every vampire in my vision as Bourne and Griffin accepted a tin of black paint and two paint brushes from Lorn's satchel. Were they going to vandalise the building? Redecorate?

"It's the seat of mortal power in this country," Lorn explained freely, seeming almost pleased to be asked. Or maybe for the chance to gloat; the man did love the sound of his own voice. "It'll make our message hit even harder."

"Our message being..." I prompted, taking a few steps closer so I could see what the other men were doing when they crouched, brushes dripping black paint.

"Their time is over. Their power will fall, and ours will rise."

I nodded. Pretty much what I'd expected. Again, I didn't think it was necessarily a *bad* idea. We had no representation in this government building at all, no one to speak up for us, and sure we had our own council but being separate would always mean hiding in the dark. Like we were something to be ashamed of. I hadn't asked to be a vampire, but I'd been born a seer and didn't we deserve at least a few councillors in *this* building? The decisions made here affected all of us.

"What'll happen to the Orders?" I asked, watching a circle begin to form as paint-strokes arched across the ground. A little chill went through me. I'd seen sigils like this before, at portal sites Rus and I had visited. I had no interest in getting anywhere near a rift to Hell again.

"They'll move in here," Lorn explained reasonably, his hands in his pockets as he watched Griffin and Bourne work. Avoiding getting his own hands dirty as usual.

"And work in tandem with the mortal MPs?" I asked with a little smirk that told him I already knew the answer. "If we oust them completely, they'll revolt."

Lorn shrugged. "Let them."

"It'll be tedious to have to fight their hunters, and whatever military they send our way."

"That's what I said," Griffin remarked with a wink in

my direction. "Waste of time fighting all those men with guns."

"And women with guns," Ember—the white-haired twin—said, appearing out of nowhere. Even I jumped at her sudden appearance. Her sister walked more sedately towards us, the skirt of her dress swishing around her ankles. "Gone are the days when women would be harmless and easy to defeat."

She sounded annoyed by the fact.

"It'd be more tedious to work *with* them," Lorn said with the air of an oft-repeated argument. "All that debating and discussing."

"Much faster to just murder them all," I quipped, uneasy as Bourne and Griffin began to paint esoteric symbols within the circle.

"Exactly." Lorn beamed at me. "You really have changed, Karina."

I didn't tell him I was being sarcastic. "I didn't realise we were opening a portal. I got back from Hell days ago; I'm not keen to return." That was putting it *very* lightly. I had to fight a shiver as I remembered that place. My stomach twisted into a double knot.

Lorn's eyes glittered, and I got the sense he saw my discomfort even as I tried to hide it. All at once, I wanted to run home to the house on the banks of the Thames, to keep running until I was in Lazarus's arms where I was safe. What the hell was I *doing here*, with Lorn of all people? What was I doing with a group of vampires who wanted to open Hell and let all its cruelty and evil into London?

He doesn't want you anymore, a merciless voice reminded me in a hiss. *He wants the old Karina.*

The truth hit me like a brick to the stomach and I sucked in a sharp breath. Too vulnerable around these predators. Aspen was watching me now, a smile on her face. Not the friendly kind.

"It's not opening on Hell," Lorn said after a long moment where he enjoyed my discomfort and fear. "Some bastard closed off the whole network to Hell, and it's gonna take us months to reconnect it."

"Maybe even years," Bourne grumbled, getting back to his feet with a glare so deep at Lorn that it sent a chill through me. I had no doubt this time that it was the demon looking out through his eyes; the temperature spiked, a stifling heat pressing against me, and I swore I saw the bright embers of fire in his blood-red eyes.

"Do you happen to know anything about that?" Lorn asked me casually.

If I said no, I'd be immediately suspicious, so I moulded the truth, my eyes on that circle drawn in black paint. "Lazarus got a call last night from a woman called Vala. She and a male demon were the ones who closed them."

"What's the demon's name?" Griffin asked with a lazy smile. But there was nothing lazy about the look in his eyes; that was sharp and intrigued.

"Not a clue," I replied with a shrug. "I didn't care, so I didn't ask."

"Interesting," Bourne murmured, as if I'd told him more than I intended to. It occurred to me that some of the demons possessing these vampires might know the man Vala brought with her.

"So if we're not opening a rift into Hell, where are we opening it to?" I asked Lorn, a little shiver skating down my arms when he reached into his satchel again and pulled out the Codex of Fiends. Everything had started with that damn book; it was the whole reason I was dead.

"That's classified," Ember and Aspen said—at the same time. Creepy.

"A little further North," was Lorn's infuriating reply. Fine, they didn't trust me yet. I'd have to worm my way deeper into their group if I was going to unearth all their secrets. But I had time; as a vampire, time was never something I had a limited supply of.

My skin crawled when Lorn held out the demon codex to me, but I forced myself to accept it, to stroke my fingertips over its warm leather cover. I wanted to shiver, but I fought the sensation, eyeing Lorn with surprise and suspicion. Why give it to me?

"Let me guess," I drawled. "You still haven't learned how to read it?"

"Why would I need to when I have access to a librarian with an endless wealth of knowledge?" he replied smoothly, charming in a way that made me want to make gagging noises.

"What page?" I sighed. The portal wouldn't open to Hell, and my moral compass pointed in a firmly ambiguous direction so I didn't really care *where* it opened as long as it wasn't that nightmare place. I knew there was a chance this would be bad. But Lorn was testing me. The others were watching, waiting for me to slip up. And if I did, I'd never find out the true depth of Lorn's plan, never find the *others* he mentioned, and London would be overrun with monsters just like Invequius.

"Forty-four," Lorn said, looking surprised when I immediately flipped to that page and skim-read the instructions for taking command of a group of demons. I wondered if this invocation would work for the bondlings, too. Only one way to find out.

"Forgive me for pointing out the obvious," I drawled, "but to take control of demons, you have to actually *have* demons."

Lorn's smile made me uneasy.

"Not to worry," Ember and Aspen said, moving forward as one, their hair like blood and moonlight, dresses pitch like the night sky. "We can open it."

They stood at the edge of the circle, hand in hand, and began to murmur a language that made all the hairs on the back of my neck stand on end. That was no tongue I'd ever heard. It was guttural but musical, with a flow that shouldn't have been possible but sounded natural in the twins' sweet voices.

Griffin grinned, standing between Lorn and I, Bourne coming to loom on Lorn's other side, all ours stares fixed on the circle of black paint.

"Showtime," he murmured just as a flash of light cracked the circle in two and *things* began to crawl out.

SEVEN

These were like no demons I'd ever seen. Their skin resembled the inside of a volcano—bubbled and weeping viscous orange liquid that reminded me a little too much of our trek through Hell. I grit my teeth, fighting through the memories like slogging through a pit of tar. They clung to me, giving me flashes of a treacherous mountain pass, quick-moving lava, then a rope bridge collapsing, and my Aunt Jubilee plummeting into the fog. Inside my head, I screamed. On the outside, I was frozen, silent, staring.

"Start reading," Lorn barked, startling me into action.

I began at the top of the yellowed page, the words flowing far easier than they had even when I worked at the Witching Library. I'd always had a knack for languages, and I'd studied this one extensively, but it was natural in my mouth now, not wieldy and strange on my tongue. Just another confirmation that I'd changed, that Hell had shifted me into something new.

The demons jerked to an unnatural halt inside the

circle when my words hit them. There were eleven of them, all crammed into the tight circle Bourne and Griffin had painted in front of the entrance to the Houses of Parliament. Anyone in the cars driving past would see them if they looked closely enough. They'd see the ritual circle on the ground, the too-fast movements of the twins as they raced around the circle, checking for breaks. If they looked closer, they'd see my claws and horns, and the wings tucked tight to my back.

A shiver ran across the delicate membrane as I stared at the demons, having to physically force my attention back to the page, reading a passage that bound them to my will with no wiggle room for them to test my control.

I felt them struggling, fighting against my voice even as every word I spoke added a new link in the chain containing them. But I didn't just need to contain them; I needed them under *my* command. Yet again Lorn was giving me too much power, putting me in charge of the codex, but getting the upper hand last time had resulted in me bound to Invequius. I couldn't let anything like that happen again. I *refused* to let anyone else possess me.

I faltered for a second when the demons turned all at once to face me, milky eyes fixed on me and only me. I allowed a single gasp and forged on, speaking faster, reading the words with force and determination. This was a different sort of magic than the one I used on Invequius. I didn't need to speak the names of these lesser demons; by the end of this page, they'd do anything and everything I told them. But the more I read, the hotter my fire burned, until I exhaled curls of steam I worried would damage the codex.

"How much longer?" one of the twins asked.

"Let her work," Lorn snapped.

Both distractions that cost me seconds before I recovered. In those few seconds I *felt* the demons press against the circle, testing the power I'd coiled around them, searching for a chink in the armour. I could feel their hunger, their rage, too. They wanted to devour and destroy, and they wouldn't stop at us. They'd unleash their appetite on all of London.

I suddenly felt so stupid for risking this, for bringing demons here. But it wasn't Hell this time. *It's not Hell.* A group of demons could be contained. A horde could not. An army like the ones we saw marching in Hell would decimate everything in the country. It would be a wasteland, everything familiar scorched to blackened ground.

My voice hardened as I read the next passage, and I felt their flinch like we were linked. Not bound, not possessed, but connected by the Codex, the magic, the harsh words of an ancient demon language they were beholden to.

I didn't feel the cool rush of the wind, or the rain driving into my head, my wings, my shoulders, slicking my hair to my cheeks. I stopped hearing Lorn and his little gang bickering. It was like being in a wind tunnel, the yellowed vellum and the huddle of snarling demons the only things that existed. And then, deep down in my soul where I'd forgotten it was buried—a pulse of alarm, like my mate sensed what I was doing.

I'm ending this, I thought as if Lazarus could hear me. *I'm dealing with Lorn once and for all. I'll use these demons to—*

I cried out when rough hands ripped the Codex of Fiends from my grip, three passages yet unread. "What are you doing?" I hissed at the bastard himself, unable to read the expression on Lorn's face. No smugness, no surprise, not even anger.

"That's enough," he said, closing the book, but not before I saw the pages were remarkably dry despite the downpour. For some reason that of all things sent a little shiver through me, awareness of just how powerful the codex was. Lorn's voice was every bit as even as his expression, giving no clues.

"I haven't bound them yet," I argued, my temper getting the better of me. I could still feel their struggle and anger and endless hunger, but only barely, like a ghost sensation instead of a solid impression. "I didn't finish reading the page."

"That's the whole point," Bourne said with a pitying look that got my hackles up.

All at once, I felt the rain soaking my clothes to my body, dripping from the ends of my hair, uncomfortable as it forced between my collar and my neck. "The whole point," I echoed, and watched the raindrops that hit my hands turn to steam. The cool liquid rolling down my spine heated and evaporated. "You brought me here to bind these demons to your will." This I said to Lorn. "But you were never going to let me?"

"It would have been a nice outcome," he remarked, hands in his pockets. "But I'd rather use my demons to take care of an unexpected little problem."

The problem being me.

The smile that lifted my lip from my teeth made him blink. "This won't end the way you want it to."

Lorn raised a single eyebrow, already turning away, the codex tucked back into his satchel. A quick glance around said the others had gone, vanishing in the blink of an eye. Leaving us alone with twelve demons whose skin wept lava.

"We'll see," he murmured, and I understood the true test wasn't binding the demons to his every whim; it was *this,* surviving a group of demons left to rampage. Or maybe he really did want them to kill me. I watched him leave from the corner of my eye and didn't budge from my spot beside the road, eyeing the demons inside the circle.

I could have fled. Could have raced after Lorn. But whether he wanted to kill me or not, this *was* a way to prove myself, to worm my way even further into his inner circle. So I braced my feet, let fire rise in the palms of my hands, and jerked my chin at the demons.

"You can come out now."

The circle had never held them; the paint had been a decoy to trick me into thinking this was a legit task. My suspicions were confirmed when the first demon shuffled over the thick black line on the floor.

I wasn't afraid. My inferno was raging, ready.

EIGHT

In my mind, I'd fight the demons one by one, dispatch them easily, and storm back to the Hobgoblin to lord my continued existence over Lorn. In reality, they swarmed me as one, their hungry mouths hanging open on broken stumps of teeth. I suspected they would use those teeth to crunch my bones and grind my bones to small, easily digestible chunks.

I was feeling a tad less confident now.

I ducked a greedy, grasping hand that oozed thick, red pus, and swerved left—into the path of a snarling mouth. Vampire speed was the only reason I didn't get my throat ripped out; I jerked back on pure instinct, gasping down a breath of rain and brimstone-tainted air.

My claws ripped through the arm of another demon, gouging deep enough that the blackened limb hung onto its body by a few determined tendons. The blood that splashed my knuckles *burned*, forcing a hiss from deep in my throat. On my next inhale, I could *taste* the stench of them—mould and putrid, rotting things. I tried to jump back, to put some distance between me and the demons so I could come up with a better plan, but I was surrounded.

Right. *Fuck.* Two demons at my front, one to my left, one to my right, and one behind me. I threw a hand back, a giddy thrill in my belly when a streak of crimson flame leapt from my palm and erupted on contact with the demon's skin, using the lava like fuel to spread. Hot air blew my hair back from my face. The smile that bloomed across my face should have warned the demons in front of me of my intention, but they didn't slow their hungry pursuit. They paid for that mistake, stumbling back as I lit them up like tinder, violent, hungry flame pouring from the palms of my hands. These demons weren't the only ones hungry for destruction; my demon magic was *ravenous.* It made me breathless, the sheer force of that power making me shudder as it flowed from me.

I pushed an inflamed demon aside with my hand wrapped in orange flames, and set my eyes on my next victim. When the demon didn't slow, it told me everything I needed to know. They had no critical thinking, only base instincts. My smile grew, flames dancing higher, *hotter.*

The next demon that reached for me didn't stand a chance. Its oozing fingers combusted before they could even graze my sleeve, fire consuming its body until the open wounds on charred skin turned to ashes. The others should have rightly backed off, but they walked into my fire, one by one, like lambs to the slaughter. Lambs sacrificed to my power.

I filled my lungs with a breath, relishing the scent of char and flames and bubbling demon skin. It tasted like power. My smile grew, until it sat unnaturally on my face, until my body shivered with the rush of magic, until embers spat from my trembling fingers.

The seventh and eighth demon went up in flames, their eyes widening as death raced down their bodies, too fast for them to scream. There was no grief or rage from the other demons, no acknowledgement that they'd died at all. They made it easy for me, and my power grew, trembling through me.

I knew some made contact, knew claws opened gouges on my arms, my side, but I was so full of power they were like papercuts. I didn't even feel the burns left by their acidic blood, even if I saw the rashes cast across my skin in crimson blotches. None of that mattered when every demon death sent glee and magic and *rightness* coursing through me.

A demon grabbed my left horn from behind, and a sudden spike of sensation weakened my knees. My stomach dropped, sickness twisting violently as I spun, trying to rip my horn from its burning grasp. I hadn't felt the other pains but this was hot and pulsing and refused to be ignored. It brought tears of blood to my eyes and that just pissed me off. *I* was the predator here. I was the one slaughtering all of them, not the one here to be slaughtered. Birdie's taunt came back to me, the word *prey* incensing me.

I gritted my teeth, fangs grinding together, and punched my claws into the demon's gut, grabbing a messy fistful of organs and ripping them out. It barely even stumbled. The demon had found a weakness and refused to release my horn. Others closed in, their gross hands brushing my shoulders, my arms. I inhaled a slow, shuddering breath, losing control of my temper. Or maybe losing control of the inferno.

But I felt it seething in my core and I *let* it rampage, let it erupt through my skin, catching the demon who dared to grab my arm. It burned it to a crisp while I forced back the bastard gripping my horn. Even ripping out its intestines hadn't slowed it down. I gnashed my teeth again, nostrils flaring as I slashed and ripped and carved out pieces of it, fuelling fire in a sudden rush down my arm. The second flame hit the bloody hole I'd made of the demon's stomach, it stumbled back, leaving burned prints in my horn but finally releasing me.

"Bastard," I snarled, tenderly reaching for my throbbing horn and hissing on contact. It had been badly damaged but it was only a surface burn. I'd survive. That didn't stop it hurting like a bitch, though.

A shadow bled across the floor and I spun to meet the next assailant, snapping my arm towards it and thrilled when a whip of flame uncoiled from my hand and wound around the demon's throat. I'd never been a great fighter but the demon part of me knew exactly what to do. A single tug severed its head from its body, a gooey, charred head rolling to a stop against my boots. I stared in a little amazement at my own actions.

How many left? Three? No, *two,* both of them bigger than the others, as if their size directly related to their intelligence and they'd let the others run to their deaths. I flexed my hands, looking into those inhuman eyes and ignoring the bleating voice in the back of my head. That was old, mortal Karina screaming at me to run. I just broadened my stance and crooked a fiery finger at the demons, already planning how I'd kill them. My fire rushed under my skin as if it knew what I needed and was eager to enact my vision.

The tiny past-Karina voice warned that I was using magic and battling demons on the side of the street, right in front of the Houses of Parliament where anyone could see. I didn't care. It felt *good* to fight, a rush of bubbling thrill in my blood despite the pain throbbing down my horn.

And the more demons I destroyed, the safer the city would be. Any humans watching this would thank me if they realised a whole realm of nightmares wanted to break into London and take over.

I blinked, and one of the demons was close enough to snag my hair, jerking me forward a sudden step. My stomach pitched at how close those jagged stumps of teeth were, at the hot breath fanning from its mouth. Even without breathing, I knew it was rancid and my eyes watered, veiling my vision with blood until I blinked.

"Big mistake," I panted, falling back on bravado as I sank deep into the well of fire inside me and let it erupt, as crimson and rich as blood. The hank of red hair in the demon's fist blackened as my demon magic burned the bastard to a husk. I frowned at the shorter strands, at the dark scorched edges until a shadow stretched over the pavement.

"I don't think so," I muttered, aware of the last demon rushing in on my left, bent to tackle me like a rugby player. I sidestepped his clumsy move, quickly assessing his brawn, his height, and huge fists, before I shook myself. I didn't need to physically *fight* him; this wasn't hand-to-hand combat. And my magic was already ready.

A wave of crackling fire left me so powerfully that my hair blew back from my face, the demon forced back a step. The scent of burned demon flesh was so strong it coated my tongue, some remains still smoking around us; I watched the demon glance at the corpses but they didn't deter it from racing at me, shoulder angled low again. I didn't move out of its path, didn't flinch. I let it get within two feet of me before I released the leash on my power.

It devoured the last demon in seconds, and left me panting, trembling, my eyes wide with the shot of strength and power. My blood fizzed in my veins. I wanted *more*. I hadn't killed every demon Lorn was hiding; there would be more on the other side of the circle painted on the ground. I needed more blood, more fire, more carnage.

I stepped around the burning corpse of a demon and approached the black circle, toeing it with my boot. I sent an experimental rush of flame, hoping more demons would appear, but it was dead. I had to wonder if the circle had brought them here at all, or if this was all the twins' doing.

The twins. Ember and Aspen. I could burn them, too. Bourne and Griffin, too. That wouldn't ruin my plan *too* badly. I'd still have Lorn to tell me where he'd been keeping these demons. Where to find the *others* and erase them as a threat. Or maybe I could burn the truth out of him instead of waiting to win his trust. And then I could hunt down every last bondling he confessed to making and burn *them*, too.

My inferno overflowed, thrilled at the prospect, and I

gasped as heat burned the backs of my eyes, the tip of my tongue, the end of my nose. My fangs throbbed. My damaged horn screamed.

Enough, I thought at my power, trying to grasp at it, to pull it back. But it raced out of control, and sparks left my mouth when I gasped. I curled my clawed hands into fists to crush the flames from the tips of my fingers, only *barely* managing to snuff it out. When I reached inside me and imagined gripping the crimson flames, extinguishing them too, a sudden pain dropped me to my knees.

A second attempt earned me another rush of pain, forcing a gasp. And still the fire raged.

NINE

The look on Lorn's face was priceless when I staggered into the Hobgoblin's taproom, my boots scorching footprints into the sticky floor, flames dripping from my body. The walk across London had been hellish, my fire battling me the whole way, the fight to control it grinding my teeth and making my head flash with a vicious ache. The inferno wanted me to burn the heart out of every person I crossed, human or paranormal. It didn't care as long as someone died, as long as the fire could catch.

The twins startled out of the chairs they'd been sitting in, embroidering matching circles of linen of all things. Bourne took a healthy step back at the sight of the rich crimson fire flowing in erratic streams along my arms, down the black fabric of my trousers. My coat had scorch marks burned into it when I shrugged out of it, tossing it over the back of a chair.

"Wine," I said, giving Griffin a stern look and

annoyed when he grinned like the sight of me delighted him. "Red."

"Yes, ma'am," he replied with a neat salute, strolling behind the bar to pour me a glass, passing it over with a flourish.

I drained it in one go, and held Lorn's beady eyes the whole time in a clear challenge. *I know you tried to kill me. But you fucked up. Now we're playing my game.*

"Any more demons you want me to barbecue?" I asked casually.

He leaned back in the vermillion booth, propping one foot on the opposite knee. "None just yet."

"Good. Let's get one thing straight, Lorn." I said his name with a heavy dose of hatred. "I can't stand you. If I believed anyone else could make a world where we're seen as equals instead of a secret shame to be hidden from humans, I'd follow *them* in a heartbeat. I'm only here, working with you, because we have the same vision."

He tilted his head, glossy hair falling across his cheek, his whole attention fixed on me. No one else spoke. "And what is that, Karina?"

"Equality." Equal power, equal respect. "So what's next?"

Lorn's face cycled through half a dozen different expressions before he settled on something borderline impressed. I didn't buy it; I'd seen all the other options. Every part of Lorn was manufactured. "The crack we opened tonight allowed only a small group through, but it was a successful test."

"If you ignore the fact I burned them to a crisp," I input dryly.

He ignored that. Griffin snorted. "The next step is to open a wider crack, to allow more through."

"With the purpose of... destroying London? I happen to like the city as it is. You might be happy to rule a city of ashes, but I'm a fan of bookshops and galleries and pubs. Demons will destroy *everything*. Trust me, I've been to Hell. It's a wasteland."

The red-haired twin, Aspen, winced, averting her eyes. Interesting. She didn't have any marks of a Bane form, but I wondered if she'd at least glimpsed Hell to have that reaction.

"Shame you don't command enough respect to form an army of vampires," I remarked to Lorn. "They'd have no issue removing mortals from power with the city intact."

His expression turned stony. I had a feeling if he'd still been human, his face would have been purple, and I couldn't fight a smile. I tasted fire on my tongue—embers and blood and charcoal. I wondered if he could smell it on my breath, wondered if he knew I'd brought a little piece of Hell back with me.

"Don't worry that pretty head, Karina," he said, rising in a smooth flow of motion. "With your language skills and that book you died for, we'll bring the demons under our control. No rampaging necessary."

Bastard. For reminding me why I was killed and turned. Absolute bastard. I smiled, more a baring of teeth than anything. "What would you have done if the demons killed me?"

He shrugged a single, lazy shoulder. "Found someone else who could read the codex, I suppose. You've saved me the hassle." I hissed, snapping my teeth when he tapped the tip of my nose with his finger. "We're ahead of schedule thanks to you."

Ahead of schedule for unleashing demons on London. I hated him. Hated this entire idea. But I couldn't deny the slow purr of intrigue from my magic, the little voice in the back of my head that wondered if I could do it, if I could control a horde of demons.

"You snatch that book out of my hand again, and I'll fuel so much fire into your body that your eyeballs pop and your soul curls like burnt paper."

Lorn's laugh was loud and genuine. I hated that, too. "Oh darling, what makes you think I have one?"

I wasn't going to entertain that psychotic remark with a reply, but I could see Griffin winding up for a snarky comment from the corner of my eye. Whatever he was about to say died with the clatter of the pub door opening, a harried blonde girl blurring as she raced into the Hobgoblin, stopping only when she slammed into the chair Ember had vacated at the sight of me. At first glimpse, I thought the blonde was around twelve years old, but when she lifted her head, fair hair a halo around her face, I realised she was at least twenty-five but built as delicate and fine as a bird. She couldn't have been taller than four-foot-nine, and the floral dress she wore made her seem younger, too, but as a vampire she could have been centuries old.

"What the fuck, Auriga?" Griffin demanded, ruby eyes wide as he watched her grab the chair back in both hands, her small body shaking. Not because she'd run here; she was no more out of breath than I was. Because she was *afraid*.

"Did you hear?" she rasped, her voice naturally ragged, the edges raw.

"Hear what?" Bourne asked, shockingly gentle as he put a big arm around the woman, guiding her towards the banquette seating, touching her with a familiarity that told me here was another of Lorn's gang of faithful zealots.

"Keaton," Auriga breathed.

My back snapped straight, the sound of my sire's name hitting me like an electric shock to the system. "What about him?" I asked warily.

The woman lifted her head, giving me a curious glance before the panic returned to her face. "He's dead."

I PROBABLY SHOULDN'T HAVE SMILED on reflection. It was a *tad* insensitive. But the relief and happiness that washed over me upon learning my sire, my attacker, was dead was palpable. I didn't throw a celebration or pull any party poppers, so I thought my reaction was restrained and graceful.

Beneath my glee at Keaton's demise was a steadily thrumming warmth. I hadn't killed Keaton, even if I wanted to. But the giddy thrill in my stomach told me I knew who had. Lazarus. He was coming for me. And that should have hurt, or at least made me nervous, but the fact he was hunting me, cared enough to search for me, made me want to kick my feet in happiness.

My emotions kept flipping, probably thanks to the fire bubbling in my blood, but tonight was a happy night and no one could take that from me. I went up to the bedroom in the Hobgoblin feeling like the world was okay for once. Sure, Lorn had tried to kill me, but he'd failed. Demons almost broke into London, but I took care of them. My horn was burned raw and still throbbing, but it would heal. And Lazarus still cared about me. He wouldn't have killed Keaton if it wasn't a message for me.

Maybe he'd had enough time now to accept me as I was, to see I was still the woman who loved him, who'd crossed Hell beside him. I just wasn't afraid anymore. And goddamn did I miss him.

But I had a job to do, a vampire maniac to take down, and a demon plot to thwart. After that, I could go home.

TEN

Today was a bad day. The bright optimism of last night was about as far from my mind as it could get, and blackness descended over me. Not because of Keaton, or Lorn, or even Rus.

I leaned against the cold white iron of the Albert Bridge, watching an Uber Boat chug its way towards Battersea Power Station and deeper into the city. The air filled my lungs with the reassuring scent of home, the wind refreshing without raking sharp claws across my face. After last night, it should have been a day filled with victory. Instead, I choked on memories, one after another after another. All because Aspen had pulled out a tarot deck at the small table by the window in the upstairs living room to read the day ahead.

Just like Aunt Jubilee used to. Used to because she was dead, because Hell killed her, Elsabeth let her fall, Corbinian stood back and let it happen, and we'd all just *left her there*. Even though I knew she didn't survive the fall, we should have taken her body with us. We'd left her *in Hell.*

It was easier to focus on my revenge campaign against Lorn, far easier to let the hungry inferno take over, than to even glance in the direction of my loss. I couldn't acknowledge it. Couldn't risk that, or I'd be wrecked like I was today.

I bowed over, my arms resting on the railing, and closed my eyes against a sudden sting of tears. I didn't let them fall. I'd be fine. This grief wouldn't get a foothold. I just had to think about Lorn, about his plan to summon all his demons into London to take the seat of power here for himself. I just had to stay angry, and then the grief couldn't shatter me.

But it felt like my dead heart broke in my chest the more memories pelted me. Jubilee in the kitchen, humming under her breath as she made her famous chicken casserole. Jubilee tutting as she drew the tower in her daily tarot reading. Jubilee sliding cubes of steak to her huskies and telling them to keep it secret, as if dogs could speak. Jubilee giving me a sly look as she told me she'd seen a tall, dark, handsome man in my future, a twinkle in her eye.

Every memory was a direct hit to the dead muscle inside my chest, every one making me flinch until I felt warm, familiar arms around me instead of the cool ebb and flow of the wind, until I smelled her perfume instead of the Thames, exhaust fumes, and blood.

Blood?

I jumped hard, startling embarrassingly for a vampire, when something small and heavy brushed my calves. A hiss formed in the back of my throat, fangs bared as I snapped my attention down to—a plump grey tabby cat with his head cocked at an imperious angle and orange eyes peering up at me with a healthy dose of judgement. There was a drop of blood on his mouth; he licked it clean.

"Hi, Mum," Keith said, his mouth opening, cute little cat teeth catching the light.

I blinked. Processed the fact he was talking to me *as a cat* and bent down to pick him up with a sigh. "Could you speak all this time, you little shit?"

"I'm not little," he protested airily, headbutting my jaw before a tank revved inside his chest, his purring rattling *my* rib cage. "And no, this is new. Did you kill anyone yet?"

"Only demons and a bondling," I replied, momentarily struck by how strange it felt to speak of murder so casually. But the demons needed to die before they could destroy my home, and the pink-haired girl was my way into Lorn's gang of psychos. Birdie, too.

Keith blinked at my statement. "Well done," he said, and seemed to mean it. "Elsabeth's looking for you. So is Lazarus."

My stomach tightened at the thought of Lazarus's mum finding me. She didn't like me much, even though I saved her life. Or maybe I was projecting the fact I hated her after she let Jubilee sacrifice herself.

"Were you looking for me, too?" I asked Keith, stroking the spot behind his ear and smiling when his head lolled into my hand.

"Nah, I knew where you were the whole time." He

purred harder, not seeming to care there were mortals walking across the bridge who might baulk at the sight of a talking cat. "I followed you out."

"You—" I sighed, my eyes sliding shut. "Of course you did." I should have realised Keith would stalk me, should have realised he'd been suspiciously quiet that day. "Have *you* killed anyone since we got out of Hell?"

"Only four," he replied, shoving his face into my hand when I stopped petting him. "They all deserved it. Abusers and perverts. The world is a better place because I killed them."

"I thought the same when I killed twelve demons," I said with relief that someone finally understood what I was feeling... and then realised I was relating to the murderous feline who ate people.

Ugh.

Maybe I needed to re-evaluate my life choices before I started eating people, too.

"When are you coming home?" Keith asked, blinking up at me with wide, sad eyes.

"When Lorn's dead," I replied, a heaviness pressing over my chest and not because Keith leant all his considerable weight against me. I missed the house by the river. I missed Lazarus. I missed my mum and my aunt, but Jubilee was never coming back and Mum—Mum didn't even know.

"Can I eat him?" Keith asked genuinely, making me laugh when I so desperately needed it. His presence was a life preserver, the only thing keeping me from drowning.

"No," I laughed, choking on it. "You'll get indigestion."

Keith made a *hmm* sound like that was a fair point, purring up a storm. When he leaned up, pink tongue flicking out towards my horn—tucked under my hood so mortal eyes didn't see them—I flinched, expecting pain. The opposite happened. The sharp throb that had tortured me since last night eased, like he had magic saliva. Knowing Keith, he probably did.

"Thanks," I rasped, struck with a tangle of emotion.

"Your horn tastes like the vitamin powder Lazarus sneaks into my food," he complained, but settled against my chest again without further remark.

"Keith, does—" I swallowed, looking across the bridge at another Uber Boat putting its way towards us, people standing on its deck and pointing at a landmark on the banks. "Does Lazarus still want me, or is he searching for me to... to put me down?"

"To put his mate down? Karina, you've never said anything quite so impeccably stupid before."

"Thanks," I rasped.

Keith shuffled around in my arms until he could put both paws on my chest, and began kneading. It kinda hurt, especially when he got a tender spot on my boob, but I appreciated the gesture so I let him continue. "He's worried about you. Stressing is a better word choice. He keeps pulling his hair out. He thinks you'll get yourself killed. I keep telling him you can just flambé anyone who tries to hurt you, but he's in a tragic state and he refuses to see reason."

"He still thinks I'm the sweet, harmless librarian he saved."

Keith gave me a look. "The sweet, harmless librarian

he first found draining a man to death?" He snorted, putting his pink nose in the air and looking even more superior. "You've never been harmless."

"But this magic—"

"Is impressive," Keith finished, flexing his claws against my chest, "but definitely going to burn you up until you're like the blackened steak Rus served me."

I rolled my eyes. "That was *one time*. Are you really going to hold it against me forever?"

"You distracted him with your womanly wiles and he burnt my dinner. Yes, I am."

I pressed a smile between my lips, not wanting to add insult to injury. It faded when his words registered. "It's not really going to burn me up, is it?"

"Oh yeah," Keith replied, eyeing a man in a blue windbreaker as he jogged past, either deciding he was harmless or too boring to merit further observation because he faced me again. "Undoubtedly. Vampires can't hold demon magic—or at least not *this much* demon magic. It'll make you all roasted. But," he added slowly, with significance, "I promise not to eat you, even if you smell really delicious roasted."

"Uh. Thanks."

"You're welcome. Now, you need to expel some of that magic if you're going to avoid burning up. Any idea how to do that?"

My eyes were wide. "You're asking *me*?"

"You're a librarian, aren't you?" Keith gave me a look that said I'd reached new, previously uncharted levels of stupidity. "Find a book about it."

He squirmed from my arms and jumped to the pavement, his tail in the air as he trotted away.

"Keith," I called. He paused on the pavement to give me a look. "I'm sorry you had to give up your other form."

"Eh." He managed a feline shrug despite not having the muscles for it. "I can still kill things, so I don't mind."

And with that he left.

I turned back to the river and the view of the city, feeling lighter in one way but heavier in others. I hadn't believed Elsabeth when she said the magic would overwhelm me, and I'd got angry at Rus's suggestion of the same. Something about hearing it from Keith made it real.

I needed to find more information about demon magic before it killed me.

ELEVEN

As a librarian, it killed me a little to tuck three books into the inside pockets of my coat and walk out of the small local library that served the supernatural community without checking them out.

Sorry, sorry, I thought inside my head over and over as I walked through the car park and into the street, heading in the direction of the Hobgoblin. *I'm so sorry, I promise I'll bring these back.* The library was nowhere near the size of the Witching Library, but I'd found three books that seemed promising, all about demons. And of course there was the codex if I ever got my hands on it again. I made a mental note to ask Lorn where he kept it before I ended his twisted life.

I was still a little disgusted that he planned to unleash *demons* on parliament. Sure, we deserved representatives, but there were better ways to go about it. Letting demons lay waste to a whole city would hardly endear humans to us. We needed a way to gain power, to come out from the dark as equals, but this wasn't it. Literally any other plan would be better if it didn't involve demons, princes, or Hell.

I was glad I rarely got tired because the walk back to the Hobgoblin seemed to take forever. The sun was high in the sky by the time I pushed open the heavy, stained-glass inlaid door—and blinked at the atmosphere I walked into.

Griffin and Aspen seemed to be in the middle of an argument; they both turned and gawked at the sight of me when I let the door fall shut behind me.

"So only one of us is missing," Aspen said bitterly, her pale face contorted with a high emotion I didn't know her well enough to read. She was like a vengeful ghost with her moonlight skin and long red hair, with the ivory dress she wore today. "Great news."

"Who's missing?" I asked, looking around and spotting only Aspen, Griffin, and Lorn slowly rising from a seat in the corner where he'd sat pouring through the pages of the Codex of Fiends. What was he doing, looking at the pictures? He couldn't read it.

"My sister," Aspen said with a glare hot enough to awaken my inferno. My power had been slumbering since the bridge, since Keith comforted my soul. Now it rushed back to the surface in response to the threat in Aspen's glare. "Do you know what happened to her?"

I didn't like her tone, but she was usually attached to Ember at the hip so I allowed her a little grace. "If I wanted her dead, I'd have ripped her heart out in front of you."

Griffin made a face like that was a fair point.

"I saw her before I left. She was reading tarot."

Aspen's face fell; she nodded, her arms wrapped around herself. "She does that every morning and then goes out for breakfast."

Breakfast being fresh human blood I presumed.

"Where have you been?" Lorn asked, more curious than accusatory, his walk slow and prowling as he crossed the pub, leaving the codex open on the table. I itched to go over and read it but resisted its pull. Later. If I let him know I was too interested in it now, Lorn would hold it over me.

I pulled a book from my pocket. "The library."

I carefully masked my expression, even if their unease sent a little thrill through me. Lazarus had found them, was *hunting* them, was coming for me. I needed to be quick, to act before he could mess up all my plans.

"Can we still open a wider crack with Ember missing?" I asked when Lorn lost interest in me, removing a sleek phone from the pocket of his trousers, his usual suit jacket missing today, the sleeves of his crisp white shirt rolled up. That was the only outward sign of his anger. He must have known Rus was hunting him, too.

"It'll be slower, but it can be done with Aspen alone."

"I'm not doing it without my sister there," she argued, a redness to her eyes that said she was close to tears.

"Yes, you are," Lorn replied with enough authority that her mouth snapped shut on whatever she'd been about to add, her eyes flashing with hot, fiery rage. His voice thundered through my head, echoing in a way that made me wince, that made my own mouth firmly close. My tongue felt swollen and unwieldy. An icy sensation shivered down my spine, like I was out of control in my own body again, like someone else had command of me.

Invequius is dead. There are no demons here. I'm safe.

Aspen's jaw clenched like mine did, a muscle feathering in her pale cheek, her wine hair stark against her skin, not quite as groomed as usual. She'd frozen to the spot, a hand to her chest, like Lorn's voice reached into her chest and squeezed. Suffocated.

"Griffin, go with Aspen and search for Ember," Lorn sighed, like Aspen was overreacting. I swallowed. Rus had compelled me, but it never felt like this. I wasn't even the one Lorn had compelled and it felt like he'd punched me in the solar plexus. Another shiver dripped like ice down my back. He must have compelled his followers before today, but why did this time hit me like this?

"Karina, come read a passage for me," Lorn ordered casually, already dismissing the other two vampires like they were tedious.

My feet scuffed the sticky wood floor before I could even contemplate agreeing, and the cold feeling in me intensified. Aspen and Griffin were already out of the door, leaving me alone with Lorn and a rapid sense of doom.

"What passage?" I asked, swallowing down the feeling. I was my own person, I was in control, Lorn couldn't command me unless I let him. I flexed my hands, my fingertips tingling with tiny flickers of fire.

"I've tracked down the page we need, but I don't know what this paragraph says," Lorn explained, sounding ordinary and perfectly amiable as he slid back into the booth seat. I dropped into a chair across from him. "I need my command over the demons to be iron-clad. I don't want a repeat of the Invequius situation."

I shuddered before I could stop myself.

Lorn noticed. "It's also in your interests to make sure nothing else goes wrong. I don't care who the demons possess, but they need to be in *my* control. Not rampaging for fun."

"He didn't rampage," I muttered, turning the codex to face me and scanning it. A completely different invocation than the one I read in front of the Houses of Parliament. The bastard didn't even give me the right page. "He was too clever for that."

For a moment, grief surged up like water rising to my chest, then my throat, then my lips, until I could barely gasp down air. I could hear Jubilee's voice, see her face just before she jumped off the platform, smell her perfume as if she was standing right beside me.

I flinched away from the memories, putting a shutter down over my expression, but Lorn said in a voice like steel, "No. Don't run from your emotions; use them. You're angry at Invequius, so use it to help me secure a better future for our kind."

The water rose up, grief drowning me, and I pushed a hand against my chest, the codex forgotten as I struggled for air I didn't even need.

"You will be at the front of a new, better world," Lorn went on, watching me with an intensity that made my skin crawl. "And Invequius is *dead*."

"I'd be dead if you had your way," I hissed, gasping.

Lorn tilted his head, sleek hair falling to one side as he contemplated me. "That's true." He rose to his feet, peering down at me. "And that would have been a waste. *Breathe.* And read the passage, Karina."

Air rushed into my lungs, cool relief making me sag, and I *hated* that I'd shown weakness in front of my enemy, my target, my prey. I hated that he saw me as weak, as much as I told myself I could use it to my advantage. He was right about that much; I should use my emotions as fuel, use every choking moment of guilt as a reminder of what I was here to do.

So I fixed my eyes on the codex and read the words once, twice, three times until I had them committed to memory, and then I searched for a spell to stop my magic overwhelming me.

In six hundred thin vellum pages, I found nothing, only a hint of how to treat injuries dealt by demon magic, how to acquire demon magic for yourself, how to bind a demon's power, and a warning to never, ever enrage a demon prince into using theirs. Because a single hit from a demon prince meant sure and instant death. Good to know. Lucky for me, I didn't plan to ever encounter one.

I let all the noises of the pub wash over me, not paying particular attention to people walking on the road outside, chatting among themselves, a couple in the middle of an argument. Annoyed at the codex's lack of help for my magic issue, I returned to the page Lorn left me with, scanning it for any trap he might set.

It was no great jump to assume he'd use this not only to open a wider rift to allow through the small army of demons he'd gathered but, if possible, to pull them from anywhere else they might be hiding in England, maybe even in the rest of the world if he could adapt the wording of the summoning spell. At least Hell was firmly closed to him.

Too-fast footsteps made me lift my head from where it had bent lower, my nose almost pressed to vellum. That was someone running at vampire speed, and since we were the only vampires on this road...

I closed the book and rose just as the doors swung open and red-haired Aspen burst in like a tornado, throwing herself against the bar, trembling from head to toe.

"Aspen?" I asked, rushing over to her, alarmed by her appearance. We weren't friends, weren't even allies, but for a second the inferno and demonic side of me was quiet and my empathy reared its head. "Is it Ember? Did you find her?"

She shook her head, leaning over her hands braced on the bar, quivers running all the way through her, shaking her crimson hair, her white, ghostly dress. "We were searching Greenwich Park. Ember used to love the observatory—it was our secret place, so I thought she might have gone there if she got in trouble, where only I would know to find her."

"She wasn't there," I guessed.

"We were ambushed," Aspen corrected, whipping around to glare at me. "Your fucking boyfriend was there. He must have kidnapped Ember, because there's no way in hell she would have set me up and led him there."

I blinked. It was the most I'd heard her speak. "Lazarus ambushed you?"

"Yes," Aspen spat, fangs bared. "It took me two hours to lose the prick."

"Well," I said, returning to my chair and my codex. "There's some good news for you. Dead women can't talk, so your sister's definitely alive."

"I'd kill you if Lorn hadn't forbidden it," she snarled, animalistic and threatening.

I yawned, turning the page, my back to her. One false move from her and she'd go up in flames. "Good thing he needs me to read from this book," I replied, that brief flash of sympathy gone.

"You're not even going to ask where Griffin is?" Aspen demanded.

I turned my head to scan the room. Huh. I'd forgotten the smirking, irreverent man went out with her.

"Well," I prompted. "Where is he?"

The look Aspen gave me was downright hateful. "Lazarus got him."

The fear in her voice was palpable. Even Lorn's followers were afraid of the Shadow Bringer.

"Huh," I said, and turned back to the book, hiding a smile.

TWELVE

I'd plotted a slow, subtle corruption among Lorn's cabal, planned to sow seeds to turn them against each other, but Lazarus hunting them did all the work for me. I should have felt a little bad for them. I'm sure I would have pitied them before Hell. Now, I just glanced around at the lush, verdant foliage of the Old English Garden in Battersea Park, hiding my smile from the cabal who walked beside me.

There were more of them tonight: Lorn walking with his nose in the air and confidence like a cloak around him, Aspen sour and gloomy in a ragged black dress with her hair in knots down her back, Bourne as calm and unreadable as ever, Auriga in another floral dress that made her look about twelve, her expression thoughtful and distracted.

And behind us came five others I hadn't bothered to learn the names of. I mentally called them Baseball Cap, Snake Tattoo, T-Bird, Gangster, and Scarlett Johansson, their names fairly self explanatory. None of them looked enthused about our location despite its beauty, natural arches of foliage hanging over the path we walked. I supposed we weren't here for a relaxing nighttime walk. We were here to summon more demons from wherever Lorn had stashed them before the portals to Hell all snapped shut.

If I'd been smart, I would have asked Vala and her demon boyfriend how to wipe out every demon here in London while I was closing the portals. They probably wouldn't have told me; it would have affected her demon boyfriend, after all. It wouldn't have done anything about the bondlings walking behind me anyway. I sensed their power, my skin itching with warning of their infernal magic. I didn't like the way my fire danced inside me, like it wanted to come out to play. It was hard to forget the way I'd barely kept control over my magic in Westminster, the urge to let the flames devour every last living person almost too irresistible.

It wouldn't get like that again. This power was mine to control; it answered to *me*.

I lifted my head when we reached our destination: the Victorian bandstand at the heart of the park. I winced at the thought of anything happening to the beautiful green columns or any of the filigree details, but demons would destroy anything regardless of its history. I doubted any of the trees surrounding it on all sides would survive, either. But it was my job to keep them in control *if* Lorn allowed me to finish the incantation from last time.

But that was a problem for later.

I accepted the Codex of Fiends when Lorn handed it to me, eyeing him warily as he gave out hard commands, directing his minions to stand in a circle in front of the bandstand, the strange mix of people lit by sparse light from the moon and distant streetlights. This felt a lot more serious than the last time I read from the codex; this felt like a ritual. That sense only grew when Lorn's clipped voice commanded blood to spill, and wrists thrust forward, sharp fingernails carving through skin, others ripped open with fangs.

My hands shook, his command crawling across my skin until my sharp fingernails bit into the yellowed pages of the book. I killed my breathing to hide the fact I wanted to pant. It was like back at the Hobgoblin but stronger, as if my body was *frantic* to obey his command even as my mind screamed at it to disobey.

There were no pretty circles painted on the floor this time, only puddles of blood that ran in rivers to pool in the middle of the ground. When it grew big enough to satisfy Lorn, he locked eyes with me and said, "Begin."

I'd already opened it to the right page. I tried not to be daunted by the two full pages of tight, slanted writing. I could do this. But I struggled to remember why I thought helping Lorn was a good idea, especially when this would allow his small army of demons into the city. Looking at the ritual, I wanted to turn and run.

But Keaton was dead. Lorn was starting to trust me. I could do this. After, I'd be fully entrenched in his cabal; I already knew most of his plan. I just needed to know how many more demons he had hidden, waiting for a crack to open, and then I could end it. End him. I could go home.

I was so close.

But there was a part of me that wondered if I could do

more. If I could *use* these demons instead of killing them, if I could unleash them on the armies I'd seen travelling through Hell and wipe out the entire species. The idea was so appealing that my arms covered with goosebumps. I opened my mouth and read the first line, and told myself it was my choice. Deep down, I wasn't sure how much was because I wanted to read it and how much was because Lorn's compulsion crawled down my spine like claws of ice.

Again, the words rolled off my tongue too easily, the demon magic that filled my veins because of my bond with Invequius making it no effort at all to speak words I'd never learned to speak. Even though I'd never heard them before I knew my pronunciation was flawless. If fire hadn't rushed to fill my body, flickering with excitement, I might have experienced a trickle of cold at that. Knowledge took years of learning and study; that was the natural way of things. Instant knowledge like this was unnatural.

I kept my eyes on the codex as I finished the second paragraph of cramped writing, fighting the little flinch that wanted to rock me when Lorn said, "That's enough blood. Take a step back."

My fire faltered a second when everyone took a step at once, like they were choreographed, only Lorn and I not moving. It rushed back twice as hot, twice as fierce, when I finished the next passage and the blood pooled in the middle of our circle exploded into rich, crimson flames. I must have flinched this time because Lorn spoke in the smooth, cold silk voice I hated. The voice of the man who threw me across the library and left me for dead.

"This is supposed to happen. Keep reading."

I could feel it then: the hot pulse of demon power, the brimstone and ash of demon blood. My stomach cramped. *I'm not in Hell,* I hissed at myself and kept reading, my conviction slipping with every word I read, until I was sure I really didn't want to do this. But if I stopped now, Lorn would kill me. Just an hour ago I'd been so convinced I could kill him, kill all of them, but doubt crept into me like poison.

"The ground will split open and demons will come through," Lorn said, either speaking to me or the others. "Karina, you'll take command of them instantly. Page forty-four."

I swallowed my panic and nodded. What the hell was I doing here? *Killing Lorn,* I reminded myself. Finding all his demons, wiping them out, and ending his evil life before he could do any more damage. I needed my inferno to scorch all that doubt from my mind, needed the sharp edge of confidence I'd had in Westminster.

I hesitated over the last paragraph. My stomach whirled, roiling like a dark sea.

"*Read,*" Lorn commanded, tearing a gasp from my mouth.

My mouth moved, sounds leaving my tongue without my permission. My eyes stung. Rage poured through me, feeling a lot like strength, like the confidence I lacked. How *dare* this bastard take command of me? I wasn't his to compel. *I* was the one with demon magic. I was the one who could read this codex. He needed me, not the other way around.

But no matter how angry I got, even with my nostrils

flaring and each word bitten out, I read all the way to the end of the spell. Fire itched under my skin, hungry to devour but ... locked inside me. I was lucky to not singe an ancient book like the Codex of Fiends but... why was my fire trapped under my skin?

I shot Lorn a mutinous look. He'd done something, commanded me without me realising it. The little smirk on his face when I bared my fangs confirmed it.

I would have attacked him and not given a shit if it fucked up my plan, but the ground rumbled, shuddering under my boots. My stare snapped back to the pool of blood just as it burned up.

The ground bubbled and *split,* tearing like an earth-quake had ripped it apart. With a gasp, I stumbled back three steps, my eyes widening when the others held their positions. Right—Lorn hadn't commanded them to move.

The spiky sense of panic that I was doing the wrong thing only grew when long spindly white fingers clawed at the jagged edges of stone and heaved themselves out of the chasm. There was no circle to hold them this time. There was nothing to stop them destroying the band-stand, the park, nothing to stop them coming for us.

"Page forty-four, Karina," Lorn commented idly. "In your own time."

Fuck. It wasn't a command this time, but that did nothing to dispel the ice of my unease as I flicked franti-cally through pages. Without hesitation, I launched into the invocation from Westminster, syllables smooth and lyrical and entirely too at home on my tongue. The cold grew, dousing my flame. Or was that Lorn, fucking with me? He wanted me as a tool to use, but he didn't want me *too* powerful. He must have guessed I was planning to stab him in the back.

"They don't look right," one of Lorn's followers remarked, his voice like velvet thunder. Gangster, I thought, the mid-forties guy in a black coat and fedora. "What's wrong with them?"

"Good question," Lorn said, sliding a glance at me.

I shrugged, reading as fast as I could, aware of more and more pale figures clawing their way out of the ground. *They're your demons,* I wanted to say. *I just opened the rift.*

"Someone must have tampered with them," Lorn said, scrutinising each and every one of us. His eyes lingered on Aspen; she held his stare with contempt. Good for her if she'd fucked with his demons. That took the heat off me, and distracted Lorn long enough that I'd read half the page in a couple minutes, halting the demons where they were, just metres away from me. I felt the magic lock into place, each word a link in that chain binding them to my will, just like last time.

Unlike last time, I refused to stop until it was done.

I tried not to look at the demons too closely, but there was something *wrong* with their elongated, milk-white bodies. Lupine limbs stretched, tipped in claws at their hands and feet, faces full of teeth and eyes—too many eyes. Legs stuck out at odd angles like bones had been snapped, others missing limbs, some with heads hanging off their necks in grotesque ways. Like white wolves who'd escaped a radiation disaster.

I ripped my stare away and fixed it on the ground, but that wasn't much better. More and more clawed their way into Battersea Park, until there must have been fifty white, broken demons pushing their way into the circle.

I shuddered, waiting for my fire to explode in reaction to my fear, but it never did. Motherfucker. My inferno was my main advantage against these people—and against the demons as more and *more* filled the circle. Seventy now. Or maybe there were a hundred. How many demons did Lorn have stashed away? Jesus.

"Something's wrong," Bourne commented, his low voice quiet. "They're fighting the spell."

"Louder, Karina," Lorn snapped, and my whole body jerked as the words struck, my rage and panic rising in equal measure as I began to shout, crying out the last few passages exactly as Lorn commanded.

This couldn't be allowed. I *refused* to be compelled by another evil monster. I would not be a victim again. Not with this much fire, this much magic. I hadn't gone through Hell and dragged myself back, lost my—*that* wasn't for nothing. Lorn didn't get to win.

The last line erupted from me with every last bit of that rage. *I command you to obey under the name of Hell and Lorn.* That's what the line should have said.

I got a rush of fiery satisfaction when instead I said, "I command you to obey under the name of Hell and Karina Dobrev."

THIRTEEN

Big mistake.

I knew I'd fucked up the moment a hundred milky white demon heads snapped towards me, vaguely lupine with ears that stuck up from smooth skulls. There was an oozing sense of malice about them that made me want to back up, but they were under my control now. They were *mine*.

"Undo it," Lorn barked, breaking the circle and rushing me at vampire speed. I snapped my arm up to stop the arc of his hand, earning myself a deep gouge in my forearm, but it was better than my throat.

I met Lorn's eyes, my soul shrinking away from the pure evil in them. "I'll undo it when you give me my fire back."

He laughed, his upper lip curled in a sneer. "You don't need fire for this."

"You have *no right* to take it from me," I hissed, my voice not remotely human. "You have no idea what I went through for that fire. What I *lost*."

I had the distant sense of the circle breaking around us, Lorn's cabal watching us, but they didn't attack me so I shut out the warning creeping down my spine.

"Undo it," Lorn commanded, his voice so rich, so compelling, that it pulled at my soul, made every cell in my body lean towards him until it physically *hurt* to resist. Pain pounded between my ears, gathered in my clenched jaw. My tongue stung when I bit it. "Put them under my control."

"Fire," I bit out, the only word I could say with the lead weight of his compulsion pressing on me, no longer silken, not even prickling and cruel like I'd felt earlier. This was brute force and blunt trauma and I felt my bones bow under it, my fangs gnashing, cutting my lip.

"No," Lorn spat. "Give me control of them and *then* I'll return your magic."

More and more compulsion piled on the first command, ripping a gasp from my lips at the sheer power of it. My hands had locked around the codex but now they shook, trembling uncontrollably. My fingers were too heavy, moments from finding another incantation to release the demons from my control. But I couldn't. If I did that, Lorn won. If I did that, he'd never pay for killing me, for putting me on Invequius's radar, for what happened to Aunt Jubilee. He needed to pay.

A hiss tore from me, my fangs bared in his face, longer than they'd been when I first transitioned. His fault—all of this was *his* fault.

"Boss?" someone asked, a hoarse female voice I barely recognised. One of the new ones. Snake Tattoo maybe.

"Release them," Lorn compelled with enough force

that my knees buckled and I hit the ground, frantically clutching the codex to my chest. Tears burned my eyes, blood dripping down my face, and I became aware of matching trails leaving my nose, my ears. Cold where they should have been warm.

"Fuck," I snarled, spitting blood, "you."

My head was full of pressure, throbbing so loudly that I couldn't *think,* but I opened my mouth again and spoke.

"Kill him. Kill Lorn. *Kill him.*"

My fire flared in response to the guttural howls a hundred lupine demons let out, a horrible orchestra of wickedness and violence, but the scalding power was a *relief.* I bowed over my knees, digging my claws into the ground, cutting through stone, trying to haul myself to my feet.

"What did you do?" Lorn demanded. I'd spoken in the demonic language. He didn't know a single word I'd said. *"Undo it,"* he commanded, throwing so much power into his voice that I whimpered, pain slicing through me like a scythe's edge. I couldn't move, couldn't lift my head, and I could no longer speak, but I'd done what needed to be done.

"Fight them, you fools," he snapped, presumably at the cabal, though I couldn't see anything except the ground and Lorn's shiny shoes as he crouched in front of me and grabbed my hair. A harsh yank had my head lifting. More pain, this time flashing across my scalp. "What did you *do,* you little bitch?"

I hurt too much to speak, to move, but I drew on my rage in order to smile. It was all I had, that smile, but I watched the impact of it hit Lorn. His nostrils flared, true rage, true murder in his eyes. Fear skittered down my spine. He'd kept me alive to do this ritual, because I was useful, but now I'd proven I didn't care to obey him... he would kill me. And this time he wouldn't leave me to a horde of demons; he'd get his own hands bloody.

A sharp cry of pain drew his attention, breaking the painful eye contact long enough for me to choke down air. It didn't help with the agony but it did clear my head enough to spit out, *"Obey your ruler,"* drawing on the old words in the codex. *"Don't stop until Lorn is dead."*

Enough demons had attacked the cabal that Lorn left me on the ground with a shove, recognising the danger to his own life. Without him looming over me, the pain lifted a fraction—barely, but enough for me to drag my legs under me and stumble to my feet.

I faltered at the carnage in front of me. I don't know what I'd expected, but it wasn't black and crimson fire streaking across the park, catching trees on fire, while vampires clashed with white lupine demons, vampire speed meeting its match in twisted, elongated bodies that moved in eerily jerky motions—but fast. Faster than I'd expected. My breath caught. I tasted it then: demon magic. Brimstone and iron and blood. Not from the lupines Lorn had collected, that I'd taken command of, but the *bondlings*. The cabal. Not a single vampire was home right now; the demons were in command.

Ice went down my spine, memories breathing down my neck until I could hear myself screaming, feel the helplessness and rage of being trapped inside my own body while Invequius piloted me.

Not here. He's not here.

But Lorn was—and he was running, leaving his cabal to be slaughtered while he saved himself.

"Coward," I yelled, surprised to find I could speak again, that I wasn't wavering on my feet, that I was *stronger*. I reached for my fire, but my heart sank when I found the block still there, leaving me with only a trickle to fight with. But the proximity of the white demons was giving me strength. The scent of Hell, the thick cloud of brimstone in the air, the hot, sticky feeling of it, that all gave me strength.

Lorn paused—and turned. Slowly enough that my blood iced over. Demons and vampires hissed and bled and fought between us, but I didn't look away from Lorn.

"They're getting away," Bourne yelled.

"Let them," someone else snapped. "We should be running, too."

"Fight to the death," Lorn commanded, his voice like a whip cracking the ground. I flinched but didn't look away. The order hooked into me too, muscles tightening in my legs, my hands curling into fists. I'd dropped the codex when he compelled me, and while part of me wanted to make a grab for it, this command was too powerful to ignore. My soul buckled, powerless to disobey and—Keaton was dead. That was why Lorn's compulsion hit so hard. Keaton was dead, which made Lorn my direct link, still my grandsire but entirely too fucking powerful.

Fight to the death he said? *Alright, asshole. You really should have specified who I was to fight.*

He saw me coming. Let me blur through a pool of blood and dismembered limbs, let me race across the bandstand, vault the railing, and land in front of him.

"Come to die, Karina? Are you so eager to be reunited with your aunt?"

I flinched, just like he wanted me to. I couldn't block the images, the sounds—Jubilee's eyes crinkling as she smiled, her head thrown back with a loud guffaw of laughter.

"Fuck you," I snarled, my voice deeper, rougher. The demon magic in the air might have strengthened me but my whole body still fought his first command. I refused to release control of the lupine demons. Even now they fought the vampires to get to Lorn. I didn't know how many had been killed, but surely enough were alive to kill the bastard in front of me. I just had to stall long enough for them to deal with the cabal Lorn used as a human shield. "How do you know about her?"

I couldn't say her name. I tried to, but it sank hooks into my throat and refused to emerge.

Lorn raised a judgemental eyebrow, looking me up and down like there was nothing remarkable about me. "My cabal is made of demons. I know everything."

My hand was already curled into a fist; I swung it into his gut, the crunch of his bones satisfying. "Did you know I was going to do that?"

Lorn only laughed, as if he wasn't in pain. Maybe he wasn't. "You're predictable, Karina. I knew you'd slip up and betray me given the opportunity."

"You murdered me; we're hardly best friends." I watched him carefully, waiting for the strike. Because he would strike.

"I don't doubt the tragic passing of your dear, dead aunt shattered you, but people like you never lose your sense of right and wrong. You're only here on Lazarus's orders."

My laugh was rapid and sharp. "Wrong." I swung at him again and hissed when he grabbed my wrist, squeezing hard enough to grind my bones against one another. "I came of my own volition. Rus hunting your minions is a nice added bonus."

Lorn bared his fangs, his true ugliness on display, all the sleek civility he usually hid behind stripped away. Good. He should be true to himself in his final moments. "Bullshit," he spat.

"Really," I laughed. "You're far more obsessed with him than he is with you. He barely even talks about you."

I was getting under his skin. I could see it.

"I'm not sure why you're gloating, Karina," he said, matching my laughter, neither of us turning to see what caused the sudden eruption of demon shrieks. When Lorn stepped left, circling me, I matched it right. "Lazarus disowned me because I had a different vision for the world. Do you think he'll have you back after all *you've* done? Letting demons loose on London—twice?" He tutted. "He'll never accept you."

"Oh, shut up," I sighed, pretending his words weren't a thorn in my heart. I'd had the same thoughts, over and over.

He moved another step; I matched it, a bright orange flame in the edge of my vision, making my stomach churn. The park was burning down around us.

"Lazarus doesn't want a world where we're accepted. He's perfectly content in the dark, living in fear of rats with no power themselves. But you? You're not in the dark anymore, Karina. You're out in the open, in Battersea park commanding demons, unleashing fire on the Thames."

I gasped, twisting my head—and freezing when I saw the river was ablaze. The demons had set fire to *the Thames*. Fuck. Oh, holy fuck.

"He'll never have you back now. He'll shun you like he did to me. He'll look at you with the same shame, talk about you with the same disgust."

"*Shut the fuck up,*" I snapped, dragging my attention from the fiery river to see Lorn had crept closer. Much closer. I threw my arm out to block his messy grab.

"He'll lock you up, throw you to the council," Lorn laughed. "You're fucked now, Karina."

I hated him, hated every disgusting drip of poison from his mouth. I hated that he was right. Rus would never have me back now. He'd turn me over to the council, lock me in the cell where Keaton died. But I'd only ever done all this was to keep demons out of my home, to kill Lorn, to stop him putting me through Hell again. I wasn't evil for evil's sake like Lorn. I ignored his platitudes about wanting a better world; as much as I wanted that too, Lorn would never be the one to make it happen. He was too selfish, too cruel. He'd be a dictator. We'd be worse under his rule than under human rule.

"I don't need him to accept me," I panted, and wished Lorn couldn't hear the pain in my voice. "I don't need anyone to accept me. I just need you dead."

Lorn came for me so fast that even when I twisted aside, his hands tangled in my hair, dragging me back. Pain snapped across my scalp. It was still sore from earlier but now it blazed with agony. A grunt ripped free when his fist drove into my ribs hard enough that something cracked.

Tears blurred my eyes again, veiling my vision in red, but I felt the air shift and lunged to the left, choking back a cry of pain. *Fuck,* it hurt, like dagger after dagger driven into my side. Blood fell from my eyes, tracking down my face, and I had to bite my tongue to kill the urge to give in, to hand over command of the demons to Lorn. If he weakened me any further, I'd do exactly as he compelled me to. And then he'd have whatever remained of the demon horde to do with as he wished. Take over parliament, control London, control the whole country.

Fuck that. Not happening.

I swung my hand around and raked my claws through his side, twisting until I gouged deep, painful craters in his side. He grinned, flashing fangs. Flames spat and snarled behind us; the heat of it grazed my skin as it jumped from tree to tree, setting the park ablaze, but I didn't dare look away from Lorn. I felt it wrap closer—death. His or mine, I couldn't say, but it settled over me like a shadow, making me shudder.

I punched my claws into him again, getting his chest this time, but I choked when Lorn's own hand locked around my neck. He squeezed with all his strength until my eyes bulged, until it hurt so much I cried, until I felt my throat collapse. I parted my lips to command the demons to obey him, but no sound emerged. My stabs and swipes grew frantic. My hands were covered in blood, Lorn's stomach a gory mess. He squeezed my throat harder. I didn't *need* to breathe, but every instinct I had screamed that I was going to die. I'd survive a collapsed throat, but if Lorn ripped my throat *out*...

I looked into his smug eyes and beheld my own death. Cold doused my insides as panic mounted, my hands frantic as I pushed and stabbed to get his hand from around my throat and—

Blood hit my face, hot and coppery and so sweet that with pain ravaging my body, making me feral, a hiss tore up my bruised throat. I licked my lips, the taste of his blood making my mouth water. I needed more, needed—

The hand had left my neck, had fallen away and it took me a moment to realise why I was covered in blood, why Lorn wasn't wrecking my throat.

Someone had torn him away from me, had ripped his head off his neck. My eyes blew wide, pupils dilating, breath quickening as I stared. It wasn't a demon, wasn't one of the cabal who'd killed Lorn. It was Lazarus.

FOURTEEN

The compulsion lifted me from so suddenly that I wavered, the grip on my lungs releasing so I could suck down horrid gasps of air. Blood and iron and scorched wood—the taste of it overwhelmed everything else. Without the weight of Lorn's command crushing me, every injury crashed into me, every gouge and slice and wound that oozed blood. My ribs howled true agony, slicing through my middle so painfully that I whimpered. My eyes filled with tears, veiling my vision in red, but it was enough to see Rus bare sharp, vicious fangs in a guttural hiss. He threw Lorn's head aside where the fire devouring a tree caught it, scorching his precious hair.

I stumbled back a step, struggling to process the sudden shift from Lorn crushing my windpipe to his head being ripped off to Rus holding his decapitated body upright so he could drive fist after fist into it in a purge of violent rage. Pure wrath tightened his face, his dark hair pulled into a bun, making his features even more severe, the white shirt he wore already drenched in blood.

I began to shake. The sight of Lazarus was *painful,* worse because it was such a relief to see him when I'd been so sure I was about to die. I clamped my mouth shut to trap the sob that formed. I was alive. Lorn was dead and I was *alive.* His head had already gone up in flames, infernal fire devouring it faster than any mortal flame, yet there was no erasing the brand of his fingers around my neck. They'd been one second away from ripping out my throat. Blood trickled over my collarbone, itching a path down my chest as I backed up, caught between relief and spiralling panic as Rus beat the dead body of his progeny.

He came for me. I knew he would, but the sight of him was still a shock, especially with demons clashing with vampires behind us, the park going up in flames. My hands shook harder; I fought to pull in air as Rus grabbed Lorn's arm and with a breathless show of strength, tore it off. Blood erupted, but Rus was already reaching into the pocket of his blood-dark trousers and drawing a stake. The next second, it was buried in the chest of Lorn's headless body and I jumped back another step when Rus let the inanimate body drop. There was no coming back from that—decapitation and staking. Lorn was finally, truly dead. Another shiver skated down my arms.

He'll never have you back. He'll shun you like he did to me. He'll look at you with the same shame, talk about you with the same disgust.

My head rang with a dead man's words, but they were true. I hated them, but they were *true.*

I backed up another step, my whole body trembling, pain sparking in my throat, my ribs. A loud crack made me flinch; a tree collapsed behind the rotunda, crashing to the ground. I needed to look behind myself, to see how many of the cabal had survived, to see what they were doing now they were freed of Lorn's command. Each one had a demon; even with Lorn dead, that left a lot of bondlings. Plus the lupine demons. Fuck, *I* had command of them.

"Karina," Rus said in a voice as cold as iron.

I flinched, a gasp catching my throat.

He'll lock you up, throw you to the council. You're fucked now, Karina.

Rus had found me *here,* in a park where a rift had opened up allowing a demon horde through, working with the cabal who followed Lorn's every whim. I was as dark as Lorn in his eyes, every bit as evil. And he'd done *that* to Lorn, ripped his head off.

There was no space left in me for logic, and if there was a voice in the back of my head whispering that he was my mate and I was safe, *finally* safe, now, it was too quiet. It was drowned out by panic. That panic flared like a river bursting its banks. When Rus took a step closer, fleeing was instinct. I turned and ran as fast as I could.

Demonic snarls muddied in my ears as I ran through the melee, catching flashes of fire in the corner of my vision. Bourne grappled with a white, malformed demon. Aspen was smeared on the ground with her heart ripped out and eyes open, forever staring. Baseball Cap made a run for it, pursued by a lupine with too many eyes and teeth. Those were the only bondlings I saw. Either the others were dead, too, or they'd fled.

I jumped aside when a demon swung its many-eyed head towards me, white mouth unhinged and its too-long arms reaching for me—until its eyes connected with mine and it shrank away with a howl. I didn't stop to question my luck that taking command of them apparently meant they couldn't hurt me; I kept running, fear pushing me faster, making my legs shivery and weak. I made it out of the park to the river, faltering for a moment at the sight of the water consumed by vicious, ember-red flames. What would humans think when they saw this? There were only so many things that could be blamed on climate change, and the Thames being on fire was not one of them. Was my mum in another part of London staring at this fiery river? Was—no, Jubilee wasn't staring at the river. We left her in Hell. Left her to *die* there.

The thought made fury eclipse my fear for a single moment before a heavy weight descended on my chest and crushed all feeling out. I stumbled into the railing of Albert Bridge, gripping it so hard my claws scraped the iron, my body bowed under the weight of that pain. It hurt worse than anything Lorn had done to me, hurt worse than anything I'd felt before. The heat from the river hit my face, making my skin prickle as I gasped for air. I was distantly aware of others on the bridge, of cars abandoned so people could stare at the Thames, phones recording the apocalyptic sight, voices a low drone in my ears.

I jumped when a hand fell on my shoulder, my stomach twisting as fear hit me harder than anything else. I shook so hard my teeth chattered. But I would fight. I had claws, and the tips of my wings were razor sharp, and when I reached for my magic, infernal fire raced through my veins, forging me anew. I raised my hand to fight whoever had cornered me and...

My bottom lip wobbled dangerously.

"I took them from him," were the words that escaped my swollen throat.

Lazarus's fierce expression from the park was gone, only deep, aching concern on his face. His hair was wild, tangled around his shoulders, his eyes hollow and... pleading. He wasn't attacking me, but that didn't mean he wouldn't let the council lock me up.

Words spilled from me, jagged and gasping, my whole body trembling with the need to *run*. Something held me in place, welded my feet to the bridge, and I couldn't look away. "He wanted control of the demons but I—I changed the wording and I stole them from him. He wanted to use them to take over London, but—"

"Come home," he asked hoarsely, grabbing the railing behind me but not before I saw his pale hand shaking like mine. "Don't run, Karina. Don't run from me again."

He'll look at you with the same shame, talk about you with the same disgust.

"Why?" The word burned my tongue as I spoke, but it was there in my head, screaming so loud. *Why* did he want me to come home when he didn't even like me now? "You don't know what sort of person I am. You don't know anything I've done—"

A laugh burst from Lazarus, lifting his upper lip from his fangs, the sound twisted and on the edge of madness. "I don't care, Karina. I don't give *a fuck* what you've done, I never did. Did I judge you after Vauxhall Bridge? Have I ever once cared? And why would I? Do you know the number of atrocities I've committed? Do you know how many people I've slaughtered?"

My face tingled, burned. I couldn't compute his words, didn't understand. "But you—you want to take my magic away. You looked at me like you hated me."

"I was *terrified for you.*"

Lazarus's other hand slammed onto the railing, caging me. My stomach flipped, but I couldn't take my eyes off his face, that frantic edge, that desperate *plea* in his eyes. He was right; he hadn't judged me, not ever. He'd offered acceptance and understanding at every turn and I—I didn't understand why.

"I was watching you change in front of my eyes, Karina," Lazarus said, his face closer than it had been seconds ago. "And after you closed the portals—"

I made a sound in the back of my throat. I remembered the way he looked at me, the sound of his voice that night. "You were disgusted by me."

He'll look at you with the same shame, talk about you with the same disgust.

"You said Lorn was right, Karina," Rus sighed, a weight to his voice, his shoulders dropping.

"He is but—not like this." I looked at the Thames, the burning park. "I never wanted any of this. I just wanted him dead."

Lazarus was quiet enough that I darted a look at him, finding him watching me. "Lorn was working for members of the Shadow Council to, we think, replace mortal government with ours."

I scoffed. "He was going to let his demons slaughter all the humans in charge."

"And is that what you want?" Rus asked very carefully.

"I don't want us to be hunted. I don't want demons, or Hell, or threats of humans using their armies to mass slaughter us when they find out we exist. Because they will."

"They haven't for hundreds of years."

I shook my head with a ragged laugh, though nothing was funny. "And in an age of camera phones and livestreams and social media—how long do we have, Rus?" I waved a hand at the people on the bridge, the crowd the fiery river had drawn, all of them with phones lifted to capture the sight. "I don't want demons in my home, I don't want MPs murdered, I just want—"

I didn't know. Didn't know how to put this fear into words.

"A future where you're safe," Rus murmured with a sigh.

I glanced away, emotion hitting me with deadly force. I needed to hold onto my anger, my inferno. I couldn't feel *this*. It was too big, too painful.

"So what now?" I forced myself to ask. Even the threat of Rus looking at me the way he had that night was better than the emotion lurking under my rage. "You lock me up in the dungeon? Throw me to the council?"

"The council who harbours the traitor behind all of Lorn's actions? *That* council?" Rus shook his dark head, his jaw clenching. "Come home, Karina."

"And then what?" I pressed, that emotion suffocating me now. I couldn't stand it.

"And then we try to figure out some way to stop this before London becomes Hell 2.0."

Everything faltered for a moment—my thoughts, my feelings, every motion and process in my body. "But Lorn's *dead*. I know the bondlings are still loose but—"

"Lorn was never the brains behind this operation. He was a tool. And you're right, he's dead. But there are others, and his death won't stop them for long."

"But it's over..."

It had to be over. I *needed* it to be over.

FIFTEEN

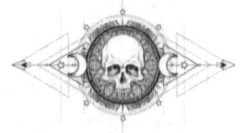

I wanted to run. The urge to burst into a sprint and flee across the city made the back of my neck itch and my feet burn. I cut off my breathing so it wouldn't race, forcing myself to walk calmly, slowly, matching Lazarus's pace.

"You didn't feed?" he asked, not taking his eyes off me for a second, like he could feel the need to flee pulling at me.

"Once," I said, my eyes fixed ahead, my mouth dry, fangs suddenly throbbing. Another pain added to the chorus of them in my body. "One of the bondlings. I broke into her house to question her about Lorn's whereabouts."

I waited for repulsion, for shock or anger or something. Disapproval, maybe.

"You broke into someone's house?"

"Yes."

Lazarus made a noise. "Impressive for a librarian."

I whipped my head around to give him an incredulous look.

"Stop expecting the worst of me," he said, which was not at all accurate. He expected the worst of me. "I've never once turned from you and I'm not about to start now. You must be hungry."

"Don't," I rasped. I could almost smell his blood. I felt it running down my throat. But I was too fragile for what he'd offer, so close to breaking that I could feel the sobs collecting in my throat, my eyes stinging as I looked at the river. It had stopped burning at least, but I knew there were demons wreaking havoc elsewhere. I didn't know how to call them, how to command them to stop. I'd left the codex in the park; it was probably burned to ashes by now. "I can't."

I couldn't handle the intimacy of feeding.

I jumped when his hand wrapped around my wrist, fingers warm on the place where my pulse ought to be. "I can feel your pain, baby vamp."

I glanced away, that pain he felt digging deeper, gnashing its teeth into me until my heart bled. "This didn't go the way I expected."

I'd spent every day since I left building up this reunion, conjuring the look in his eye from the night I ran but worse, always worse. To have Rus speak gently, handling me with obvious care, not running from me, not detaining me... I didn't know how to handle it. Couldn't fight the urge to cry.

"What did you expect?" he asked, watching me. I felt his gaze fixed on me but didn't dare turn back to him. I was a tiny crack, a very slight nudge away from falling apart. The whiplash of fighting Lorn, expecting to die, and walking along the river with Rus holding my wrist turned my emotions brittle.

"I thought you'd lock me up, for starters," I said, swallowing when my voice emerged thick.

"Don't think I haven't contemplated it. If I have you under lock and key, you can never escape me again. But no, I won't lock you up. I'll simply never take my eyes off you."

"You'll still be my jailor," I murmured, a lump in my throat.

"Jailor?" Rus's laugh was abrasive. "Oh no, not your jailor. Your extremely possessive, clingy mate who *refuses* to lose you again."

Guilt joined the caustic mix of my emotions. "I thought you'd lost interest in me. Now that I have this magic, and after everything in Hell... I thought you didn't want me anymore. You told me to get rid of my magic, but it was the only thing that made me feel strong, and I—I'm so fucking tired of feeling weak, Rus."

He tightened his fingers around my wrist, pulling until I stopped beside him, the river frothing on the other side of the wall. "I didn't handle Hell as well as I appeared to. No. As well as I *pretended* to." Now it was his turn to look at the Thames, avoiding my stare. "I'm an old bastard and I've seen a lot, but near death after near death is enough to disturb even a relic like me. You're not the only one affected by the Crucible, Karina."

I frowned, dragging a fang over the inside of my lip. "But you were fine."

His laugh assured me he was not. "I was barely holding it together. I see you and Isaiah plunge off that fucking lava pass, over and over again, even with my eyes open. When I blink, I watch Mum fall to her death and I watch you risk your life saving her. I see Jubilee fall, and I hear you scream, and I can feel your pain here." He knocked his fist against his breastbone. "I'm not handling it well, and my fear is all-consuming, and I took it out on you by ordering you like your superior when I should have listened to you as your mate."

I dug in my fang so hard it sliced my bottom lip. "I won't give up this power, Rus, not all of it. The fire's part of me now. I feel... better, with it."

"I have no right to talk about power," he replied, his eyes downcast, watching where his thumb stroked a line of fire across my wrist. "I have my own dark power as the Shadow Bringer. I wasn't trying to take it from you, or even judging you for it when it wasn't your fault you have it in the first place. I was just—afraid."

He didn't look happy to be admitting it, which made me smile. "Afraid of what?"

"You almost died every single day in Hell. We made it out by the skin of our fucking teeth."

"I never understood that phrase."

"And when Mum said the power would burn you up, that no vampire was supposed to possess that much demon magic, it triggered the fear worse than anything. Mum's warning was my final straw."

I looked at Lazarus, really looked at him, and the brittle feeling in my chest worsened at the sight of shadows clinging to every plane of his face, his eyes bleak, shoulders slumped until he looked a good few inches shorter than normal. I thought I was the only one haunted by Hell, terrified it would happen all over again, scared that we'd never truly escaped that danger. I thought Rus was fine; he *seemed* fine.

I sighed, rubbing my tired eyes with my free hand. "You didn't tell me you were struggling."

"I prefer denial to speaking about my issues, and then I just hope it all goes away. I might tell everyone else to be open and communicate, but I don't practise what I preach."

I sighed again, this one deeper. "So, to recap. I thought you were so disgusted by my new strength and my magic, and you didn't want me. And you were so afraid to lose me that it made you a control freak."

"Not the words I would have chosen," he murmured. "But that's about the gist of it."

He really was in denial. My shoulders dropped, a knot relaxing from my chest. "I'm going to get control of my magic. I know the dangers of keeping it, and I've been looking for a way to manage it. But I needed to come to that decision on my own."

Rus was watching me now, his gaze intent. "If you can believe it, your stubbornness is very attractive to me."

"You're mad, so yeah, I believe it." I forced my eyes up to his face, my stomach swooping at his soft, hopeful expression. "I'm sorry I ran away instead of talking to you."

"I'm sorry I snapped instead of talking to you." His thumb swept across my wrist, soothing the brittle edge of my feelings. "It turns out I'm very sensitive to the suggestion of losing you. I'll blame it on the mate bond."

My smile deepened into something more genuine, a little wry. "Can I do that with all my problems, too?"

Rus's hand slid, very slowly, down my wrist to my hand, interlocking our fingers. "I don't see why not. It's a convenient excuse."

I looked from our linked hands to his face. "Is this real?" It seemed like a fever dream, though my imagination tended to conjure nightmares instead of dreams. "Are you absolutely sure you don't want to shout at me that I'm an abomination or something similar?"

"Did I ever once call you that?"

"Every day in my nightmares."

"Well. Let me be perfectly clear." He waited until I made eye contact. "You are not an abomination. You're mine."

"I'm not sure those things are mutually exclusive..."

"*They are.*" His voice left no room for argument. Warm fingers tightened around mine, tugging me closer.

Lazarus didn't find me abhorrent, didn't care what I'd done in the time we'd been apart. He still wanted me. This was fucking with my head. I couldn't stop smiling. "I planned to kill Lorn, you know. Once I'd found out where he was keeping the rest of his demons."

"His demons." Rus's smile sharpened into a smirk. "What a liar. Those demons never once belonged to him. The demons were brought here by the traitor in the order. They simply gave Lorn access to them. With commands to follow, I presume."

So everything Lorn did was guided by someone in the

council. Rus was right. He was a fucking liar. I slanted a look at my mate. "You killed Keaton."

"I did."

"For me?"

"For you," he agreed.

"And Lorn?"

"That was purely selfish." His smile was all fang. "I enjoyed it."

"I saw." I stepped a little closer, a weight falling off my shoulders at his proximity. "Rus what are we gonna do about the park on fire? And the demons who got loose?"

"Isiaiah and Quinn are handling it. Will's around somewhere." It was strange to hear their names, to remember there were other people caught up in this. I'd expected to see Will in the Hobgoblin eventually; the first time I met him, he was pretending to be buddies with Lorn. I wasn't sure if Rus's snarky progeny would have made my job easier or harder.

"You make it sound so simple," I remarked dryly. "As if a hundred demons—"

"What are *you* meant to be?" a man slurred, leaning far too close to me for comfort. The scent of lager and sweat hit my nose, turning my stomach until I nearly threw up. "You Batgirl? Issa Comic Con on?"

I shot Rus a panicked look. After everything that happened, I forgot my wings and horns were on display. How many people had noticed me, but not been bold enough to remark on it unlike the drunk man now squinting at my wings?

"Forget you saw her," Rus commanded, his voice low and seductive, dragging a shiver down my spine.

The man's ruddy forehead creased. "Saw who? Nice meeting you, pal." He patted Rus on the shoulder, not noticing the blood all over Rus's shirt, or else thinking he'd got into some sort of pub fight and decided it was normal.

I waited until he staggered off, gripping Rus's hand. "I think we should go home now."

SIXTEEN

I'd forgotten the exact scent of the house on the banks of the Thames. I'd forgotten the weight on my chest fell away at the first drag of that sandalwood and musk scent. The next morning, I was still filling my lungs with it, the rarest aromatherapy—the scent of home.

I ran my hand over the back of a velvet brocade chair in the library I'd missed so much, my heart full of a strange mixture of happiness and pain. I shouldn't have run away. But Lorn was dead, and I'd managed to take out some of the demons—whoever the demons really belonged to—and at least I knew their target now: the mortal parliament. I didn't know when they'd strike, or how many demons they had, or where exactly those demons were kept now, but I told myself it was positive. We had more advantages and information than we'd had before. It was worth leaving Rus, leaving home behind.

Speaking of Lazarus... I shot him a wry glance as he

followed me across the thick carpet towards the shelves crammed with aging leather spines.

"You were serious about not letting me out of your sight, I see," I remarked, a flutter of warmth in my belly. Not fire or inferno for once—true pleasure. All last night it took me off guard, how happy I was when I'd been so prepared for heartbreak and pain when my path finally crossed with Rus's. I should have known better. I should have realised he was just as messed up by what happened in Hell as I was.

"How in control of that fire are you?" he asked, not acknowledging his clinginess. Not that I minded. At all. "Should I be worried about you burning down my library?"

I turned with a gasp, my hand flying to my chest. "How dare you. I'm a *librarian;* I would never damage books." I felt bad about the three I stole and would never be able to return from the Hobgoblin. But *burning* books was sacrilege. "I've never been so offended in my life."

Rus's smile sank deeper at one side, a little crooked. If I'd had a heart, it would have skipped. I was sure his constant hovering would get old fast, but after days of being on constant edge around threats and enemies it was nice to be so close to someone I trusted.

"Did Isaiah and Quinn manage to put out the park fire?" I asked, glancing sideways at him when his phone vibrated. He read the message without replying and slipped it into a pocket of the black sweatpants that told me we weren't venturing outdoors today. Good. I'd had enough fresh air and scorched Earth yesterday. I dreaded turning on the TV and seeing the news about Battersea Park.

"They got most of it out and then firefighters arrived," Rus replied, giving me his full attention. "Mum and Corbinian have found six of the Lyxayan demons."

Lyxayan, so that was the name of their species. "How bad is it?" I asked with a wince. "How many people are dead?"

"Three humans and a bear shifter. It could have been a lot worse."

Especially since only *six* demons had been found, and only god knew how many were left out there. A hundred or so had come through; the cabal managed to take out some, but there had to be fifty left. Maybe more.

"I don't know how to command them again," I admitted, browsing the spines until I found a small burgundy volume on mediaeval demons. I cracked it open, scanning the contents table. "Without the codex, I don't think I can give them another order. If I could, I'd forbid them to ever hurt anyone."

Rus took the book from me, flicked to a chapter near the back, and put it back in my hands. "There's nothing here about managing demon magic," he said, skimming his knuckle down my cheek. "I've checked every book I own, and several from the Witching Library." At the sharp look I shot his way, he quickly added, "I sent Will to get them for me."

"Good," I huffed. The last time we were there, council lackeys attacked us and Rus was hurt so badly he was knocked out for hours. "I had three books back at the Hobgoblin but I never got to read them."

"We'll find something," he swore, as if he could promise that. "There might be a way to call the demons to you without the codex. Mum was working on something with Corbinian; I'll ask her about it when she comes later."

My teeth were bared, a hiss in the back of my throat before I could stop myself. Lazarus blinked in surprise, then coiled a lock of my red hair around his finger, disarming me. "I know he's a demon, but he's safe to be around, Karina. He's nothing like Invequius."

I just shook my head, not wanting to explain my deep, searing hatred of his mother. The mother he dedicated *years* to finding. I was grateful she hadn't moved back in here in the time I'd been gone; she and her demon boyfriend lived across the river in Belgravia.

"I know," I bit out after a pause, trying not to crumple the book in my hands. "So what's their plan? How do I command the demons? The sooner I do it, the faster they stop killing people, right?"

Lazarus didn't answer for a moment, and I found him watching me with a gentle expression on his face.

"What?"

"I was wrong when I said you'd changed," he murmured. "You still care about people as much as you did before Hell. You still want to do the right thing."

I shrugged. "It's not completely selfless. I don't want my home ruined by demons. I thought it was over with Lorn dead, but I've had the night to come to terms with the truth." Ideally, I'd send them all back to Hell, but that would involve opening the portals again and no, thank you. Not happening. "If I can compel them to cause no harm, I can find a way to cope with them being in the city."

Lazarus's warm palm moulded to my cheek, the comfort instant. "The council won't allow you to keep fifty demons in the city. Not unless you release them into their control."

I scoffed. "And play right into the hands of whoever summoned them in the first place? I don't think so."

Rus's smile this time was even sharper.

"You have a plan, don't you?"

"A very blunt one," he agreed. "Opening the rifts to Hell isn't an option, and neither is you keeping them. You'd be under constant scrutiny. So we end them all."

I leaned against the shelf, closing the book in my hands. Rus was right; there was nothing useful for me in here. "Your solution is murder."

"It's never failed me before."

I shook my head, replacing the book and browsing the rest of the shelf. "My first impression of you was right—you are a scary psychopath."

He made my breathing skip with a soft kiss to the top of my head. Those easy, casual touches fed my soul after too long apart. "I thought you liked me because I'm a scary psychopath."

I gave him a look.

Whatever he was about to say was interrupted by a voice calling down the hall. "Rus? Where are you?"

"In the library," he called back, not seeing the way my whole body stiffened.

Elsabeth was here. The woman who let my aunt throw herself to her death, who pretended to be sympathetic after, who never even *once* thought to sacrifice herself despite having lived multiple full lifetimes. She did *nothing* to stop Jubilee, nothing to save her.

There was no controlling the hiss that rattled my throat at the sight of her, dressed in a smart blazer and trousers unlike the last time I saw her in leather. Her wings and horns were nowhere to be seen. She looked like a high-powered lawyer, not a deadly vampire so old that she'd sired Lazarus. I tried to remind myself she'd saved him, that he loved her, but seeing her flipped a switch on my composure until my fangs ached to sink into her skin, to rip her head off like Rus did to Lorn.

The look she returned was unimpressed, her gaze fixed warily on me as she approached Rus, squeezing his arm in greeting. "How long has she been like this?"

Lazarus shook his head, confusion pinching his brow. "She hasn't. And don't talk about her like she's not here. What's going on, baby vamp?"

My nostrils flared. I didn't take my eyes off Elsabeth, one moment on replay in my mind: the moment when my aunt fell to her death, when Elsabeth did *nothing*. She was a vampire older than anyone I'd ever met. She could have *saved her*. Hatred and rage and sharp, jagged grief filled my chest until it hurt too much to look at her. I ripped my stare away, panting.

"She knows I'm a threat to the demon magic she's carrying," Elsabeth said with a blend of worry and disapproval.

"Fuck you," I spat. "I want you out of my house."

Her condescending laugh grated my composure to shreds. "This is my home. I lived here for centuries before you were even born." My twisted laugh made her sigh. "I'm not trying to fight with you, Karina. I'm trying to help."

"Trying to help." My voice turned bitter. "Trying to take *this* from me more like." I flicked my fingers and flame danced along my skin. "Is this what you want?"

"You're so possessive of the power," Elsabeth murmured, disappointment in her face as she shook her head. "It's more advanced than I feared. The demon power is already corrupting you."

"I'm not corrupted," I spat, fine hairs standing on end when she came closer, a clear threat. *"Stay right there."*

"Mum, this isn't helping," Rus muttered, resting his hand on the small of my back. "Karina was fine. She's in control."

To prove him right I let fire raze higher, filling my palm, still very conscious of the books.

"I can help you," she offered, holding my stare.

"I don't want or need your help." I closed my fist, extinguishing the fire. "I just want you to leave."

Elsabeth gave me a look and transferred it to Rus. "Unchecked, she'll run out of control. She needs to purge this magic."

"I'm aware, thank you," I bit out, my nostrils flaring when she came closer, watching me like I watched her.

Whatever camaraderie we'd shared in Hell was gone. Here was the ancient vampire, the woman who'd sat on the council for decades, who was used to getting her way. "Rus, can you give us a moment? I'm a Bane, too. I can handle this."

My upper lip curled, fangs exposed. *"Handle* me?

Like you handled Jubilee? Oh, I'm so sorry there's no fatal drop you can push me into. You must be *so* disappointed."

"I never—" Elsabeth straightened, the hostility leaving her face all at once, her eyes brightening with something like comprehension.

"Rus, don't let her burn me," she said casually, striding across the room towards us, looking at me too closely. I squirmed, then jumped when dark magic rolled from her and brushed my arm. I backed up a step with a hiss, knocking her hand away. "I see."

"Back the fuck off," I snarled.

"I will in a minute. Show me your fire."

"Mum, this is—"

"Shush," Elsabeth huffed, steady, patient warmth in her expression when she regarded me. "Show me your fire, Karina."

I didn't understand her whiplash in personality, but if that's what she wanted... I let infernal magic flare in my palm, so hot it burned deep, electric blue.

She jerked back with a hiss, the ends of her very hair seared. "You should be burning up. But I wonder... you weren't human before you transitioned..."

"Mum," Lazarus prompted, impatient, when she trailed off.

Her eyes were bright as she regarded us both. "No ordinary vampire is supposed to hold so much demon magic, but Karina had magic *before* she was turned. Your control is remarkable," she told me.

"Thanks," I said flatly.

"But you hurt my son when you left, and I don't

appreciate that. And yet... you're hurting too. Karina, what happened to Jubilee—"

I snapped my fangs at her, lurching forward. Elsabeth backed up several steps and gave Rus a pointed look.

"You're actually in control of this power, likely because you're used to handling power as a seer," Elsabeth told me, but her eyes remained on Lazarus. "But this grief will destroy you unless you face it."

"Get out," I snarled, lunging at her even as the library faded. I saw Jubilee fall, heard her last words, her voice clear in my memory. It was enough to make me buckle, gripping my chest. It *hurt*. I didn't want to forget her, but I couldn't stand this pain.

"Emotions are heightened and volatile in your first year as a vampire," Elsabeth said, her voice so different, so abruptly kind, that I halted in the act of reaching for her with sharp, gleaming claws. The look in her eye, the softness of her tone... it had me drawing up short, that brittleness I'd experienced last night with Rus by the river returning. A hundred prickles stabbed my sensitive eyes, and a low buzzing started in my ears. "I've known fledglings struggle to contain even ordinary emotions, let alone endure everything you have. Getting trapped in Hell would be enough for even a seasoned vampire, let alone experiencing such a brutal loss."

I swallowed hard, my throat closed off. I didn't *want* this. It was easier to face her suspicion than her kindness. I wanted to curl into a ball and scream and shut it all out. Instead, I turned away from her and headed for the library door, the back of my neck tingling at having such a powerful vampire behind me. I could only do it because

Rus was there too, and deep down in my soul I knew he'd keep me safe.

"I would have saved her if there was any other way, Karina," she said behind me, making my fangs gnash together. "Your aunt was fatally poisoned, already destined for death, and I would never disrespect the difficult choice she made by stopping her. She gave what was left of her life to save us, and I have nothing but respect for her."

"*Stop,*" I snarled, ripping the door open and throwing myself down the hallway, air racing past my shaking body. I didn't want to hear it. I didn't want to remember, or to let the pain in. Once I gave it an inch, it would *destroy* me.

I ignored the quiet fear that it was already destroying me.

SEVENTEEN

"Hey, do you want this bird?" Keith asked, trotting over to where I'd hidden in a sitting room around the back of the house, gilt-edged furniture, sapphire upholstery, and verdant splashes of plant-life everywhere around me. I sat on the floor with my back to a sofa, gazing out the double glass doors that led to the small yard behind the house. By all rights, Keith shouldn't have been able to find me, but that didn't stop him dropping a red cardinal at my feet. It was clearly dead, but absent of blood except for a tidy incision on its throat.

I might have had red streaks of tears down my face, my hands might have been shaking, and I might have been filled with fire and fury because it was the only thing staving off my grief, but I wasn't about to turn down a gift. I remembered Keith bringing me a mouse before, and how proud he'd been of his kill. He was every bit as puffed up now, his chest stuck out and orange eyes bright as he nudged the bird towards me.

"Thanks," I rasped. "This really helps."

He nodded sagely and climbed into my lap, turning away from me so he could make biscuits on my knees. "Does this help too?"

I pushed his tail out of my face, but there was the tiniest urge to smile. "Your butthole in my face? Not really."

Keith huffed, pressing his claw deep enough to catch my skin. "I'll have you know, many a lady has been grateful to be presented with my backside. But no, I meant this." He stretched his back, walked a circle on my lap, and curled up there, dialling up a purr that made my bottom lip wobble.

"Yeah," I said, choked. "This helps."

"Word on the street is you're not being completely devoured by your magic anymore," he said, blinking up at me, the sight of him speaking still fucking weird. "Congrats."

I flexed my hand, calling fire along my fingers, the magic surging immediately, then retreating when I curled them into a fist. "I felt it respond to the demons in Battersea Park. My magic changed. I didn't notice because I was too afraid, and then Rus found me, but... I think it's settled."

"Hm." Keith yawned. "Didn't you read from the Codex of Fiends?"

"I did," I said with a frown. "Is that important?"

Keith shrugged lazily, butting his face against my stomach, purring up a storm. "You corralled all those lyaxan demons, and read an incantation to pull their power under your control. It probably worked on your magic, too."

I blinked—and blinked again, my grief interrupted for the moment.

"Holy shit," I breathed. "You're right."

It made so much sense. I'd taken control of the demons present—*all* the demons present. Including my own magic. "But what about the demons possessing the bondlings?" I asked Keith, looking down at him—and smiling at the sight of him dead asleep, his mouth parted to show teeny tiny teeth between his fangs.

I ran my fingers through his fur and let my mind run, the thoughts productive for once instead of destructive. But I kept coming back to one thing—I needed a way to call all the demons back to one place, where I could read another invocation to forbid them doing harm.

Oh yeah, and I needed to actually *find* that invocation.

I scraped a fang over my bottom lip, coming back to the same thing every time. There were more dangerous, ancient books in the library where I'd found the codex. Other books that might grant me the ability to end all this before the traitor on the council enacted their backup plan.

I needed to go back to the Witching Library.

EIGHTEEN

"Hold your breath," Isaiah said, frowning as he stared very intently at me. I squirmed, well aware that he could look at me and read every truth I was hiding—from others and *myself*—with prolonged eye contact. But there was no way around it, so I forced myself to look back at him and cut off my breathing.

"I don't like this," Quinn muttered. Isaiah's and Rus's friend had a bitter expression on her tanned face since the moment she saw me. Probably because I'd brought trouble and volatility into Rus's life. Although Lorn being his progeny and also a power-hungry maniac had nothing to do with me.

"You don't like anything," Rus said with a faint smile, his eyes on me.

Quinn harrumphed, her sharp white bob slashing around her face when she turned abruptly away from me, pinning Lazarus with her signature glare instead. I'd known she was dangerous since I first met her, but now I knew she was a seventh-generation gatekeeper, and immensely powerful. Not someone I wanted as an enemy. Unluckily for me, everything that happened since Hell had made her dislike me even more.

"Ignore them," Isaiah said, concentrating on me until a tingle of power washed over my face. My fire reacted, demon magic leaping through me, heating the underside of my skin, but I curled my hands into fists and held it back. I kept expecting it to soar out of control, to demand more destruction, more burns, more blood like it did that night at Westminster, but it really had settled. Keith was right; the codex had done this.

"There," Isaiah said with a nod, brown hair swaying around his face as he tilted his head to consider me. "Sorry about the nose, but needs must."

He handed me a mirror and moved onto Rus, repeating the intense eye-contact he'd subjected me to. My stomach still squirmed, the feeling that he'd seen right past every wall into the heart of me impossible to shake. I knew he was a dark mage, but I didn't entirely know what that meant, what *made* him dark. Sometimes I got the sense Isaiah could do things even regular dark maji couldn't.

The unease from that thought might have spread if I hadn't glanced in the mirror and startled at the brown-haired, tan-skinned woman staring back at me. Her eyes were a medium shade of brown, her face oval, nose a little bulbous, hair straight and lank. Plain and unremarkable. Isaiah had done that with a bit of eye contact and a murmur under his breath.

"Impressive," I remarked, lowering the mirror and

watching him work on Rus. The face I loved so much began to mottle and change, his skin tone deepening to a honey shade, his eye shape subtly changing, jaw rounding, irises shifting to grey-blue, nose elongating until he was utterly unrecognisable.

"You look like my nemesis from the corner shop," Quinn said with a purse of her lips. "At least no one would look at you and know it's you. I presume you're wearing a supermarket brand coat instead of a designer label."

Rus shot her a horrified look that slowly bled into betrayal as he realised the wisdom of her remark. If we wanted to be unnoticed, we needed to look normal. Designer coats weren't normal.

A smile touched my mouth for a moment, until an errant memory of Aunt Jubilee, Mum, and I peering in the window of a Bottega Veneta store flashed through my mind. We'd been admiring a leather bag, swapping dreams of one day owning it, until the sour face of a shop assistant appeared in the window, her fair hair pulled into a bun so severe it made her look bald and her expression reminiscent of someone eating a lemon covered in hot sauce. We'd snorted and walked away giggling at her stuck-up expression.

The memory was crystal clear, Mum's laugh and Jubilee's snarky comments so loud I heard them in the sitting room, as if they were right here with us.

"At least Karina won't have to change her wardrobe," Quinn said with a smirk.

I gave her the middle finger.

"Ladies, ladies, where are your manners?" Isaiah

chided. When Quinn and I pinned him with narrow-eyed glares at the same time, he held up his hands and said, "I said nothing. Nothing at all. Enjoy your verbal sparring."

"Be ready in five minutes," Rus cut in, saving Isaiah from Quinn's glare as she edged a little closer, silently threatening him as if they weren't best friends. "I'll go change my coat," he added sulkily.

The three of us laughed at the same time, a strange, temporary camaraderie between Isaiah, Quinn, and I. I knew what they thought of me, knew Elsabeth had spun her version of the truth, so I just sighed and went to find a coat, too. I didn't need one as a vampire, but I liked the added layer of armour.

C

I HALF EXPECTED Order Force officers to jump out at me as Rus and I walked the riverside path to the library, taking our time like there wasn't a traitor on the council who no doubt knew I'd taken command of their demons and Rus had killed Lorn. Oh, and like I wasn't guilty of an attack on Vauxhall Bridge, potentially risking exposure of the entire supernatural world. As if that result wasn't inevitable, and it didn't make sense to bring on at least the damn prime minister so we could start working with the human power players. And maybe, you know, avoid being hunted to extinction when the news finally spilled.

No officers appeared out of the air to arrest us. Whether they could arrest Rus when he was a councilman and the Shadow Bringer, I didn't know. I doubted it.

Rus squeezed my hand like he could tell I was distracted. For once, it wasn't memories of Hell and the past that haunted me, but everything that could happen in the future. Lorn was gone, but his death wasn't the happily ever after I'd been dreaming of. The cabal were awol. There'd been no more reports of demons killing anyone, so they'd gone to ground. There were too many unknowns.

"Look at that," Rus said with a sound in the back of his throat. When I looked at him, he gestured at a news-stand outside a little shop most humans walked past without noticing, only a rare few with the sight giving it a passing glance. I read the headline and sighed.

THREE FIRED IN COUNCIL SCANDAL.

"You predicted this," I said, reading the frustration in Rus's clenched jaw. His face might have been unfamiliar but his expressions and gestures were pure Lazarus. "You said this would happen last night."

It was one of his theories of how the council would react—and how the traitor in their midst would handle the revelation Elsabeth and I had dropped on them. Demon armies gathering in hell bearing the council insignia. Marching for portals to let loose upon our city.

Rus left me long enough to throw a couple pounds on the stand and grabbed a paper, scanning the article. "They're all low-ranking. Scapegoats, probably."

"How do we find the traitor?" I asked, leaning closer to him as we walked so I could read the paper with London its usual noisy, grey-skied self around us. It felt so strange to be back with Rus, to be *home* instead of hiding among Lorn's cabal while I planned to kill them all, but at the same time it felt right. Natural. So easy that I felt a fool for thinking Rus would ever reject me.

"Focus on the demons," Rus replied, folding up the paper and tucking it into his inside pocket when the Witching Library rose above us, all pale columns and domed beauty. "If we pull the demons from where they've got them hidden, it'll draw out the traitor."

"Who do you think it is?" I asked, keeping close to his side as two young women, clearly students, came jogging down the steps from the library. I expected my fangs to ache, expected the thirst to slam into me so suddenly that I couldn't fight it. I could hear the steady thump of heartbeats, smell the enticing sweetness of their blood, but... I didn't want it. Since Hell, only Rus's blood held appeal to me. Even with Birdie, I only drank her blood from necessity. A frown tugged my brows.

"I have my suspicions," Rus replied, holding the door open for me, not looking nervous at the prospect of getting caught or confronted like the last time we came here. I tightened my grip around his hand at the memory, and he leaned closer like he guessed the direction of my thoughts. A kiss brushed my temple, lingering as I guided us through the main hall and into the section where I'd worked for years. With our temporary disguises, no one even took a second glance at us.

God, the smell of it was the same—yellowed paper and old ink and leather spines. A weight fell off my shoulders, the comfort of the familiar, high-ceilinged space wrapping around me like a hug even if this was the place where I'd died.

"Are you alright?" Rus murmured, lifting our joined hands to kiss my knuckles.

My eyes kept returning to the end of the hall where the bookshelves had been restored and replaced, where I'd been thrown into solid wood and shattered. "I have more good memories than bad here." There was no escaping that this room had killed me, but I'd been happy here, too. It still felt a little bit like home. "I'd rather not linger, though. Let's find a book and—"

I'd begun to walk past the row of tables to the tall, sturdy bookcases that housed the oldest books in the library, but I froze when a tall, broad-shouldered figure rose from a table at the end of the row. He looked at me like he saw through the magic, like he saw *me*. His skin was rich umber, his clothes even darker, but it was his crimson eyes I got caught on, and the lack of hostility in them. The presence of *relief* instead.

I frowned, not taking another step. "Bourne?"

NINETEEN

I couldn't say why I tightened my grip on Rus's hand when he lurched forward with fangs bared, but there really was relief in Bourne's hand and the way he was watching me wasn't hostile. I threw a quick glance around the library room, noticing a couple scholar-types browsing the stacks, another sat at the far end studying on his laptop. None of the cabal. No councillor who wanted to take over the country and murder every human who got in their way. But I hadn't really expected to find that.

Bourne had always been calm, collected when the others lost their temper. Watchful and measured.

"You need to say something or Rus is gonna rip your head off," I urged, unable to resist adding, "like he did to Lorn."

Bourne winced. "I'd prefer to keep mine attached. And I'm not here to attack you. I actually like you, Karina. You don't infuriate me like most of the cabal, and you really should have died that day at Westminster." His wide mouth quirked into a smile. "Lorn was pissed off when you returned. A vein nearly burst in his forehead."

"Lorn was your leader," Rus pointed out, something feral in his voice though he allowed me to hold him back. Waiting, measuring.

"Lorn was a spoiled child throwing a tantrum because he wanted more power," Bourne argued, leaning against the table several metres away. He glanced from Rus to me, where his gaze held. "Do you know why I joined his *cabal?*" He sneered the name like he despised it.

I stayed silent, waiting for him to speak.

"He has the woman I love," Bourne snarled, the most emotion in his voice I'd ever heard. "He held her location over me for five years. I had five more to work for him before he'd tell me where he's keeping her."

Rus sighed, his demeanour thawing *slightly*. "Did you find out where she is?"

Bourne shook his head, a tic moving through his jaw. "No. That's why I'm here—I know you used to work here, Karina, so I guessed if I spent enough time in the library you'd show your face. I want to make a deal."

Lazarus stiffened all at once, tugging me closer.

"I don't make deals," I said, ignoring the sympathetic stab in my chest. He'd lost the woman he loved, and I couldn't stand the thought of losing Rus. I couldn't face the memory of what I'd already lost. I swallowed hard, shaking my head. "Sorry. I only wanted Lorn dead and now that he is—"

Bourne slid a brown satchel off the table where he'd been sitting and I froze as he flipped it open to show a weathered brown cover. My breath hitched. "I just want to know where my girl is. I don't want London to fall, or to take over the world, or any of that insane shit Lorn spewed on a daily basis. I just want *her*." His eyes slid to Lazarus. "You're on the council. So is your mother. You must have a seer or tracker on payroll."

"We do," Rus allowed, his tone frosty but his eyes fixed on the codex. I could use it to call the lyaxan demons to me, to bind them so they'd do no harm. I could call the other demons the councillor had stashed away. We could expose them. I glanced sideways, Rus and I sharing a moment of eye contact. There was a gleam of retribution in his, as if he was already thinking about what he'd do with the traitor when we caught them. "What about the demon possessing you?"

Bourne shook his head. "There never was one. I killed the demon Lorn meant for me. I just faked possession enough times to be convincing."

My eyes widened. Bourne had never been a bondling. Shit. He'd been so convincing.

"How can you see our true appearance through the magic?" Rus questioned, edging closer to me.

"I can't," Bourne replied with a frown. "But I recognise Karina's scent—and her voice."

Ah. Maybe we should have disguised those too. "What's her name? The woman you love."

"Bonnie Tsang. She's around eighty years old, but she looks—"

"Like a perpetually pissed off teenager," Rus finished with a strange laugh.

It hit me all at once. *Bonnie.* His Bonnie—the other member of their family.

"You're joking," I blurted, staring from Bourne to Rus.

"She's not in Lorn's possession and she hasn't been for years," Rus said, tilting his dark head as he assessed Bourne in a new light. "He held her for a few months back in 2020 but we freed her the moment we found out."

Bourne staggered back into the table. His expression was unguarded, stunned. "You know her? She's safe?"

"I'm her grandsire," Rus said with a frown. "She's Lorn's progeny."

Bourne dragged a hand over his jaw, his gaze distant. "That's how he got her. That's why she didn't fight when those bastards grabbed her."

My sympathetic heart clenched again, despite being a dead organ. "Those bastards...?"

"Lorn and Keaton," Bourne spat, fangs bared. "They took her, and I've never seen her since."

"Well," Rus said, releasing my hand to cross the floor to Bourne. "Assuming she has an interest in seeing you, you'll be reunited very soon. She'll be at my house tonight for dinner. I'll tell her about you then."

Bourne looked equal parts hopeful and miserable. "She's really safe? Bonnie Tsang?"

"She's really safe," Rus confirmed.

But Bourne looked past him at me and didn't relax until I nodded. "I saw her weeks ago and she seemed fine. Snarky with an attitude problem, but fine."

Bourne laughed, his eyes closing, pain writing itself across every plane of his face. "Everything I did in the past five years was for nothing."

"Not for nothing," I disagreed, approaching. "Lorn's

dead. Keaton's gone. The cabal has scattered. That's gotta be worth something."

Bourne opened his eyes, not looking convinced, but he reached into the satchel and held out the Codex of Fiends to me. "Take it." He straightened, pulling himself back together with clear effort. "I know where to find the last demon cache. I'll tell you everything I know."

I began to thank him when a hot poker shoved through my gut. I staggered, my hand flying to my middle, expecting blood and burned skin.

"Karina?" Rus demanded, his voice dropping to a growling hiss. "What's wrong?"

I shook my head. I didn't know.

Bourne was the one who answered. "Demons," he grunted. "A lot of them. Looks like someone beat us to it and already opened a rift."

TWENTY

"Oh shit," I breathed, my mind wiped of all its panic and grief at the sight of a ten-foot-long yellow slug eating a pillarbox-red Fiat 500. Its jaundiced, slimy body convulsed, forming wrinkles along its thick throat as it made a horrible retching sound, swallowing the car bit by bit.

"Mollusor demons," Bourne said with intense disgust, his nose wrinkled. "Stronger than the lupines that came through last time."

"And they're not the only ones," Rus said, pointing ahead where winged shadows cut across the grey, drizzling sky over St. James Park.

"Why always a park?" I asked, ignoring the tangled knot in my stomach as Rus, Bourne, and I jogged across the road, traffic screeching to a halt as they saw the giant slug dragging itself jerkily across the tarmac to its next meal: a black Toyota Yaris. Its blonde, athletic driver threw open the door with a scream and ran into the haven of the tube station, her door left hanging open.

The slug snapped it off, like a palate cleanser. I gagged, my hand flying to my mouth at the trail of slime it left in its wake.

"Convenience," Bourne answered my question, slipping a knife from his leather coat as we crossed the short road that led to the park. "There are always people passing through so whoever opened the rift would go unnoticed, and a park is big enough to fit an entire cache of demons when they come through. Harder to open a rift in a smaller area like a street or public building. Plus, there's always a ready food source."

"And less chance of it being traced back to them compared to opening it in the council building or their own home," Rus added, his voice as biting as ice. That glimmer of vengeance I'd seen in the library grew into a violent darkness, and a flutter of butterflies moved among the tangle of my stomach.

"How are we playing this?" Bourne asked, easily deferring to Rus when I'd expected him to push back against any instructions my mate might give.

"We hang back and assess the situation first. I sent warnings to my network and councillors I trust, so there should be people here any minute to try to manage the demons."

"Try," I echoed, running my thumb over the stake holstered at my thigh and immensely glad Rus's overprotective edge refused to let us leave the house without an armoury of weapons on us.

"Get behind those trees," Rus ordered quietly as we crossed an eerily empty street. A glance at the left end showed another huge, monstrous slug blocking off the road, making that awful gulping, retching noise. I didn't want to know what—or who—it was digesting.

We hopped a small black fence and hurried to crouch behind a patch of trees and shrubbery. It wasn't much cover but as I bent low and peered around a trunk at the paved path that led into the park proper, I saw why hiding was necessary. Another mollusor demon had draped its slimy, yellow body across the path.

"They've blocked off the exits," I whispered, my palms prickling with heat. I reached up to tie my hair back, ignoring the pink, shiny tightness of my skin. My clothes seemed to cling to my skin, inner heat making me sensitive, the fabric abrasive. I unbuttoned my coat, leaving it folded under a bush. I'd need the range of movement to fight anyway. With a sigh, Rus followed my example.

"At least it's not one of your designer coats," I whispered, trying to lighten the mood and nowhere near successful at it. "Bourne!" I hissed when he ducked around the other side of a tree, exposed if any demon were to look this way.

He crouched beside us again after a few seconds, his usual unruffled self. "There are mollusor demons on all the paths, and those winged children have gathered in the sky around a rift glowing red. I'd estimate around two hundred of them."

"Two hundred!" I shrieked. I locked eyes with Rus, not hiding my panic.

"You can do this," he assured with absolute confidence, fitting his warm hand to my cheek. "How many did you take control of in Battersea?"

"A hundred," I said, swallowing, my mouth as dry as desert sand. If this plan was going to work, I needed to control more than two hundred. I needed to command *all* of them. Every last one. "But that was different. I had to do that so I'd get a chance to kill Lorn—"

"And I need you to do this," Rus cut in, his gaze holding mine, "so I can kill the person behind this."

He pressed a kiss to the spot between my eyes and drew back when he saw the resolution in my eyes.

"Shouldn't we capture them so they can go to trial for this instead?" I asked, jumping when a horrible screech filled the sky. It was like hundreds of high-pitched voices overlapping, like a whole legion screamed their fury.

"*No,*" Lazarus said in a voice like shadow. "I'll handle the mollusor demons. Bourne, I expect you to have my mate's back, and if I get even the slightest hint that you plan to put a knife in that precious back, I will flay every last bit of skin from your body while you're still alive and begging for a reprise I will never deliver. Are we clear?"

"I gave you the codex, didn't I? Why would I betray you?" Bourne grumbled, his brows heavy over deep red eyes.

"Are," Lazarus hissed. "We. Clear?"

"Yes," Bourne bit out.

Rus slashed his chin in a nod and glanced down at the hand I'd unconsciously twisted in his shirt.

"There are a lot of those slugs, Rus."

"And I'm the Shadow Bringer," he said with a loving smile and that gleam of violence in his eyes. "I can handle myself. You just focus on yourself. If you get even a single scratch..."

I smiled, reluctantly releasing him. "You'll unleash hell?"

"Precisely." He kissed me quickly and then he was gone, vampire speed and shadows whisking him away so fast that I couldn't reach out to stop him even if I wanted to.

Another multi-layered roar came from the winged demons and I winced, the sound making my teeth rattle, my fangs ache. "Why did you call them winged children?" I asked Bourne, trying to ignore the sharpness in the bond between Rus and I, urging me to return to his side.

Bourne's eyes were narrowed, the only sign that the screeches affected him, too. "They look like eight year olds. Like evil cherubs."

"That's not unsettling at all," I muttered, jumping hard when a weight butted into my side, making me whip around with fire licking up the razor edge of my claws.

"Hi, Mum," Keith said, blinking up at me. "Who's the stray?"

I sagged with a soft groan, lowering my claws. "You scared the crap out of me. Not literally," I added when Keith reared back with a flare of his orange eyes. "And this is Bourne. He's... sort of a friend. At least an ally. He gave me the codex."

"I can smell it from here," Keith said, trotting past us with his tail in the air, his striped grey fur reflecting the crimson light from the rift. Who had opened it? Whoever they were, they must have been able to read demon languages.

"Keith, be careful."

He made a throaty sound of scorn and disappeared into the shrubbery.

"Do you need to see the demons to be able to control them?" Bourne asked, his head tilted in contemplation.

"No." I just needed the right words spoken in the correct tone. I pulled the Codex of Fiends from its satchel and cracked it open to a page I'd mentally marked in the Hobgoblin. I sucked in a slow breath, settling my nerves, and then shut off my air supply. A horrid taste coated my senses, like brimstone and charred ruins and old, mouldy socks. I could only presume the latter came from the slugs.

Another cry came from deeper in the park, sharper, feminine. Bourne went as stiff as a rod beside me, his own breathing silenced.

"Read," he commanded, and burst out from behind the trees.

"So much for having my back," I grumbled, and began to read the incantation to pull every demon in the country to this one spot.

That was the easy part. Gaining control of them? It was going to take more than a few well-placed words. It would draw energy from me, draw *power,* and I wasn't sure I had enough.

TWENTY-ONE

The sight that met my eyes when we reached the main park path was horrific, like a twisted Renaissance painting. Rus, Isaiah, and Quinn clashed with mollusor demons that dripped slime. Elsabeth swooped through the sky, fighting the winged children as the grey clouds broke open and raindrops pelted the lake. And just ahead of us, in the middle of a circle of grass scorched black, Bonnie, Will, and Corbinian faced off against two figures in long, black brocade robes. The robed figures' hoods were pulled up to hide their faces as their hands cast complicated patterns in the air.

The ground had split, a dark, ragged chasm travelling out from the circle into the park, the split so long I couldn't glimpse the end. Crimson hellfire flickered within its depths. It wasn't a portal to Hell. I told myself that over and over, but my voice faltered at the sight of it. I'd closed all the portals, burned the network; there was no way these people had opened a doorway into Hell. But enough demons had come through that it burned with deep, crimson flame, and the resemblance was enough to make me cold all over.

I didn't recognise those robes; they weren't anything I'd ever seen a councillor wear, but there was no doubt these two people were the ones who'd directed Lorn, the architects of the diabolical power grab. If it wasn't for them, Lorn would never have needed the codex. I'd still be alive. Aunt Jubilee would still be alive.

Rage hit my system like fire meeting tinder, and I had to fight to keep my flames from scorching the cover of the codex.

I paused on the path, staring at the chasm, the robed figures—one tall and imposing, the other shorter. The spells they worked with intricate hand movements weren't for the chasm, or even the demons. When the taller one punched their pale hand through the air, I realised they were offensive spells. That explained the feminine cry, and the fact Bonnie struggled to her feet, fangs bared and a smear of dirt on her face.

The sharp scent of magic filled the air as the spell flew, and my breath jumped, my whole body tensing as my legs carried me in a sudden lurch. I saw the arc of the red magic, saw its target. It was going to hit Will right in the chest, and there was no telling what it would do. Would it knock him down, cause intense pain, or kill him?

I held onto the codex with one hand, my right palm lifted, already wreathed in flame, but Will threw himself aside with a blur of supernatural speed and the spell drove into the thick trunk of a tree. A sigil scorched into the bark, glowing with rich, infernal ruby. I swore, breathless, and ground to a halt. I'd never seen that sigil before but I knew without a doubt it was intended to cause irreparable harm. Somewhere in the distance, ducks began to scream in panic. I knew the feeling.

The next spell glowed in the air with the same sigil, this time from the shorter figure. They aimed directly for Bonnie as she rammed her shoulder into the taller figure, dragging their hand down before it could do more damage and knocking the dark hood back. I gasped so deeply I tasted smoke and scorched bark. I knew that woman, the tallest figure. I'd seen her every day for years.

I stepped forward with a frown, clutching the codex to my chest, shaking my head like it would change the picture in front of her. "Ursula...?"

At her name, she whipped her head towards me. Irritation narrowed her glowing eyes, the same expression I'd seen in the library a hundred times. Ursula was the one behind all this? My boss? But...

"Why did you need Lorn to steal the codex?" I asked, my mind scrambled. "You could have taken it at any time."

She was the head of the Witching Library. She had access to *all* of it. I'd figured a scholar had to be behind this, but Ursula? She'd always been cold and foreboding, more than a little intimidating, but she wasn't a power-hungry maniac.

She rolled her eyes at me, already gathering more power with rapid flicks and swirls of her fingers, crimson magic pooling into a sigil in front of her. "I'm not foolish enough to link myself to a crime, Karina."

"But you—you allowed demons into London. They destroyed buildings and *killed people*."

Keith brushed against my calf, a silent promise of backup. Ursula's gaze flicked to the plump grey cat at my feet and blanched. That was satisfying.

"A necessary evil," she replied after her slight hitch, utterly dismissive. My mind struggled to compute *her*, here, doing *this*. She looked the same, grey and severe and exceptionally tall, like a praying mantis—all elegance and casual violence. I'd always been uneasy of her, but there was a *slight* difference between being nervous of someone and watching them defend a rift that had unleashed two hundred demons into the sky. "It's not about the demons or Hell. It's about our society deserving better. Equality—"

"I heard all this with Lorn, thanks," I snarled, ignoring the part of me that wanted the same thing. But not like this. *Never* like this. I glimpsed a shadow behind her, moving swiftly, and blurted out the first thing I could think of to keep her fixed on me. "Did you tell Lorn to kill me?"

"I told him to get the codex at any cost," she replied with a shrug—and roared when Corbinian slammed into her. Elsabeth's demon partner pumped enough infernal magic into her that the temperature spiked. The crimson magic from the rift must have boosted his power like it did mine. He looked more like a vampire than a demon, his white hair long and poker-straight, his skin as translucent as the vellum of the codex. And that wrath in his eyes was every bit as terrifying as the first time I locked gazes with Lazarus.

"Hey you," Will greeted me, skidding across the grass to my side, avoiding the giant crack in the ground. Messy brown hair fell rakishly over his forehead as he leaned closer, a little panic in his expression. "Planning on reading that book any time soon?"

I met Will's deep green eyes, my own wide. "That's *my boss.*"

"Jesus." He tapped the codex and cringed back from it. "All the more reason to handle this demon problem."

Now it was my time to cringe. "Uh. My plan is to create an even worse demon problem," I whispered.

"Bonnie!" Bourne boomed, fury adding gravel to his voice. My head snapped up just as he collided with the smaller robed figure, crushing them into the ground like a rugby tackle.

"Bourne...?" Bonnie said in a small voice, shock making her look suddenly young. "What the fuck? Where have you *been?*"

"Where have *I* been?" Bourne demanded, hot and furious, sounding like an entirely different person as he drove the robed figure's head into the ground, rendering them neatly unconscious. The hood fell back to reveal a man I didn't know—thank fuck. He had mousy brown hair, a moustache, and a plain, ordinary face. Under his robe, he seemed to be wearing a light blue polo shirt. Not who I'd expect to be the mastermind of a plan to unleash all Hell on London. I was so confused. "Where the fuck have *you* been, Bon? I thought Lorn had you locked up. I thought he was torturing you, starving you."

Bonnie gave him a look that questioned his sanity and drove a kick into the robed man prone on the ground when he began to move. Huge and bristling, Bourne stepped over him without a downward glance and grabbed Bonnie, their height difference both cute and absurd. I thought they were going to kiss, but then Bonnie drove her knee into his crotch.

"That's for leaving me, you dick," she muttered, and spun, sinking her fangs into Ursula when my boss got too close, a spell glowing in a complicated pattern between her hands. Bonnie ripped out a chunk of Ursula's arm, sending her back with a cry, and then cast a fierce glare at her boyfriend, lover, enemy—whatever Bourne was to her. Maybe all three.

"As lovely as their reunion is," Will remarked, grabbing my arm and pulling me behind the long, draping leaves of a tree. "You need to start reading. But I want it on record that I think you're insane for bringing more demons here."

"Noted. I've got a plan," I promised him, and opened the book again, reading with sharp intention, ignoring the chill of warning down my spine. This was the right thing to do. It had to be. If it wasn't, we'd be overrun with hundreds, maybe thousands of demons and—

My whole body jolted, a gasp torn from me when pastel rainbow fractals erupted in the air around me, the first vision I'd had since I returned home. I didn't question it, even if nerves tangled my stomach; I stared into the bright shards and let the vision fill my mind.

The acrid scent of smoke and brimstone fell away, even the foul scent of the mollusor demons fading. In one shard I saw Rus roaring with rage as he drove shadow after shadow into the slug demons, throwing his hand up to rip three winged children from the sky with the same stream of darkness, then another three, then four. My chest filled to bursting, pride and love overwhelming me as he cut off the head of the mollusor and moved onto the next, clearing the park at a rapid rate.

In another rainbow shard, Isaiah and Quinn fought back to back, Quinn bleeding from the temple, unsteady on her feet, her white hair drenched in blood. I watched her collapse and didn't know if it was happening now or if it was the future reflected back to me. I smelled blood, as if I stood right beside them, tasted the bright burn of Isaiah's power as he cut through the chest of a winged demon that tried to prey on Quinn. Another demon tried to sneak up on Isaiah but *Ruby* was there, thrusting a massive goose-egg sized gemstone at the demon. The red pendant hung on a chain around her neck released a blast of black-tinged magic, taking down the demon instantly.

Ruby? My best friend? That couldn't be true; she wouldn't be here. That was *insane*.

My head jerked, eyes tracking to the next shard and I fell into a vision of Keith unhinging his small cat jaw and swallowing a black-winged shadow child whole. A shiver went down my spine. I didn't linger in that vision.

The next shard hit me like a punch to the chest. It hadn't happened yet; I could feel the certainty. But if something didn't change, this *would* happen. And it was horrific.

From a distance, through a haze of prismatic light, I watched myself stand in the middle of a storm of magic and wind, the codex in my hands as my mouth formed demonic words. It was the spell to bring all the demons under my control. Thousands had gathered, flying in the sky, crowded onto the grass, even trudging through the lake—and no matter how quickly I read or how much energy and power I gave, *it didn't work*. There were too many demons for one person to control.

I watched myself drop to my knees, heard Rus scream as my voice died. As I died.

I staggered back from the vision, hitting something solid and warm. Will? I didn't know, couldn't see because the vision was shifting, the shards showing me what I needed to do. My hands shook on the codex but I scanned the scene over and over, looking for weaknesses, making damn sure it would work.

I staggered out of the vision with a groan, my head pounding, and found Will and Keith both staring at me. "I'm fine," I assured them hoarsely. "I had a vision. I know what I need to do."

If I tried to control every demon, I'd fail. I'd die.

"I'm going to need help," I said, finding my place in the codex. "I'm going to need all of you."

I couldn't do it alone. But with Elsabeth, Corbinian, with Isaiah's magic? It might be possible. I ignored the fact it might *not* and began to read, calling every demon in the country to this one park.

Please, god, don't let that last vision be wrong.

TWENTY-TWO

I t was like waking up from a nightmare only to find out the dream had been real. Hundreds upon hundreds of demons were ripped from wherever they'd been hiding all across the country, and dumped into St. James Park. The scent of brimstone thickened until it was all I could taste as I shouted the words I'd memorised from the codex, not quite able to take my eyes off the scene in front of me.

Demons in all subspecies gathered, snarling and fighting on the grass. Other, smaller demons crouched in the branches of trees like twisted koalas. Green-skinned frog demons clung to the banks of the lake, except they were all four-foot tall. Twisted animals and humanoid creatures with no faces or too many eyes skunk and slithered across the bridge. And hybrid *things* I had no name for, that looked like they'd crawled out of some fell dimension... they all gathered in the park as I yelled, louder with every word.

The codex sat heavy in my hands. The more I read,

the more tired I became, but I shoved back my fear that said this would kill me and yelled the final passage, ripping white lupines and blackened, oozing soldiers and flying, screaming demons through the glowing crimson rift Ursula and the man had opened.

When I reached the final word, there was no standing room in the park, and our allies had gathered around Will, Keith, and I, their weapons and magic pointed outward as demons brawled to vent their fear and confusion.

My breathing skipped when the crowd of demons parted, lowering their heads as a horrible piercing *shriek* poured from them. Warning crawled up the back of my neck. I exhaled a hard breath of relief when I saw Vala, the dark-haired, golden-complexioned woman who'd helped us close the portals, striding across the park, her lover or enemy or whatever he was at her side.

"Everyone who has magic," I said, glancing back at our allies, then at Vala and her demon, "I need your help. Your *power*. With the codex, I can strip every one of these demons of their power; it's the only way to end this."

Vala's demon reared back with a snarl. She whacked him on the shoulder. "Calm down, you don't have magic anyway."

"Yes, well," he replied, shooting her a look like she'd betrayed him. "I'd prefer that not to be a permanent situation."

"Ignore him," Vala told us, glancing from me to Rus and giving everyone else a vaguely friendly nod. "Hello Karina, Lazarus, assorted people. I presume you need help."

A roar cut the park as another demon fight broke out,

and I winced at the vicious crack of a tree being ripped from the ground. That tree must have been there for years. "Definitely," I breathed, the sharp spike of panic in my chest lessening slightly when Rus moved to my side, brushing a comforting stroke down my back. I ignored the tiredness weighing down my bones. I wasn't exhausted yet; I could go on.

"I need you all to form a circle with me at the front. When I read the invocation, it will pool power from all of us. It's the only way this will work."

That was what I'd seen in the vision. The only way I survived.

Lazarus was the first to wrap his fingers around my wrist as I flicked the codex to a new page, the one the vision showed me. The illustration depicted a pale-skinned, hairless demon hunched over as a smoke-like substance was ripped out of their skin. Below it were four passages. It would take less than three minutes to read, and this could all be over.

"I'm down," Vala agreed with a shrug, flicking long black hair over her shoulder and grabbing Rus's hand. "*You* can sit this one out, asshole."

"Deep down," the asshole said to Will, who happened to be closest to him, "she really does care for me."

"Clearly," Will drawled.

I was distracted by another scream of fury from the demons—this time from aquatic demons surging through the lake, spilling red through the water.

Elsabeth wrapped her fingers around my left wrist, meeting my eyes for long enough that it made me uncom-fortable. I snapped my attention down to the codex, aware of Isaiah and Quinn joining the circle, the former with a warning look to—

"Ruby, what the hell?" I demanded.

My best friend narrowed her eyes on me. "Like I'd leave you to deal with this alone. I'm here. Deal with it."

It was such a Ruby thing to say that I laughed. Reality hit me like a slap and my smile fell. "Please be careful. Don't fight any demons."

"That's what I said, and did she listen?" Isaiah grumbled. "No."

Ruby rolled her eyes.

"I would join," Corbinian said gravely, the demon catching my attention, "but my power will be stripped with the spell."

Oh. Of course it would. A pang went through my chest, and I found it was much easier to hate Corbinian when he wasn't right in front of me, regarding me with guilt and such genuine sorrow.

"I'm sorry," I said regretfully. This invocation had no exceptions; *all* demons would lose their power.

A howl of mortal-*ish* rage sounded just beyond the trees. I jumped, my gaze flying to Bonnie and Bourne when they adopted defensive stances around the circle. "What happened to Ursula and that man?"

"Knocked out," Bonnie replied, a scowl darkening her face. It made her even cuter, not that I'd dare tell her that.

"Not dead?" Should I feel bad for wishing death on my boss?

"We did try," Bourne grumbled. He proved he really was on our side and not Lorn's—well, Ursula's—by grabbing a demon who ploughed right at us, its appearance that of a tiger who'd been flattened by a steamroller, its body eerily narrow and long. Bourne bared his fangs and ripped out the demon's throat, casting it aside to grab the next one. Oh holy fucker, I needed to read. *Now*.

"Everyone ready?" I asked urgently, watching to make absolutely sure they closed the circle before I took a deep breath, ignored the dark prickle of warning and began—

A pale, grey hand snuck close enough to scratch my cheek with the razor edge of its fingernails. I jerked back with a gasp, nearly losing my grip on the codex as I flung up a hand to stop the clawed grip aiming for my throat.

Lazarus's hand tore from my wrist, the only warning he gave before he went completely nuclear with rage. Darkness streamed down his pale cheeks, his eyes like daggers forged of blood, and fangs bared on a roar so fierce it made every vampire instinct inside me scream to *run*.

"Attack them," Ursula yelled, staggering away from me through a gap in lupine demons, her eyes wide with panic. She nearly took my head off! My own boss. Fuck.

Lazarus vibrated with rage at how close she'd come to hurting me. A little shiver went down my spine. I never even saw her coming. One lapse and I would be truly, finally dead.

Ursula backed up, but Rus was already in motion. He moved like a storm of wrath and shadows, nothing but a blur until he was there, right in front of her, snarling in Ursula's face. She didn't have the chance to blink, let alone flee. A jolt went through my whole body as Rus thrust his hand into her chest, prised apart her ribs with a morbid orchestra of cracks, and ripped out a fistful of organs.

Dark streams of living magic poured from my mate, driving into Ursula's shoulder, her stomach, her thighs, anywhere they could do damage. Blood sprayed. Without a single flinch—or a shift in his menacing expression—Rus tossed a mess of lungs and heart to the ground, where... where Keith promptly helped himself and chowed down.

My stomach roiled; I ripped my stare away, focusing on the graceful figures coming out of the spaces between demons, like they'd been hiding among the legion.

Auriga, Scarlett Johanson, Baseball Cap, and Gangster.

Ursula's words repeated in my head. *Attack them.* Fuck! They'd transferred their loyalty from one zealot to another. But what happened to the man who'd been with her, the other robed figure?

"*Stop,*" Rus commanded in a voice of shadows and violence. His magic was rife in that word, a low, violent thrum that matched the dark plume gathered around him. Something went very still inside me, my breath catching. Compulsion, thick and irresistible. I got the sense the only reason I could still move, think, and breathe was because Rus had aimed the words at *them*, not me. "Claw your own eyes out and then kill each other."

It was a horrific and beautiful thing to witness all of Lorn's cabal grind to a halt, and then turn on each other without hesitation. I cringed against the desperate urge to do the same, breathing through my mouth, taking air deep and regretting it when the stench of carrion and rot and brimstone filled my senses. With Lorn dead, Rus was their direct link, and the potency of his compulsion was clear.

With poise and baffling calm, Lazarus stepped back into the line, grabbed my hand, and gave me a steadying look as the cabal brutalised each other. I nodded, ignoring the squish of blood between our fingers as I pulled myself back together, and began to read.

I tried to ignore the demons clashing brutally in front of us, chunks of flesh ripped out with hair still attached, eyes leaking rapid streams of blood where claws had turned them to pulp. The sounds were awful, their cries mingled with snarls. The wet noises of bodies being ripped apart made me want to throw up.

The first line of the page flowed from my tongue as easily as water in a stream, and I felt the effect go through the legion like a clang. Their attention turned, rapidly, to us. Cold spilled through my chest like ice water, flowed down my arms until goosebumps covered me. I read faster, pouring intent and belief into every word, delivering it like a fact, a forgone conclusion.

"Kinkiller," one of them hissed, the voice like a rasp of paper. Another chill went down my spine but I didn't allow my tongue to falter on a single lilting syllable, reading until I reached the end of the sentence, then beginning the next with only a gasp for breath. I didn't look to see why they'd fixed their attention on Corbinian, the name they called him enough to chill me without seeing exactly which demons surrounded us.

I raised my voice, words flowing faster, harsher, and I *felt* it: the first tug on my magic, like someone had thrust their hand into my soul and yanked something out. I couldn't control my gasp, couldn't stop that interruption, but I rushed to finish the sentence and begin the next.

My eyes fixed on the weathered yellow vellum of the codex, but I had the terrifying sense that demons moved closer, winged and clawed and horned and aquatic demons all converging. They knew what I was doing. They were furious. That rage washed over me, through me, like heat from an open fire, clashing with the cold of fear inside me.

I needed my inferno, needed my magic now more than ever, but fear was like a slow drip of weakness. Every word I spoke made the tug on my soul harder, sharper, yet my fire resisted.

"It'll hurt far worse if you fight it," Elsabeth said in a tight voice like she was concerned. Probably about the legion of demons I'd called into the park who were currently closing in on us, seething that I had the nerve to take their magic. Their growls and awful, rattling snarls were louder with every minute, raising the hairs on the back of my neck.

I wanted to take Elsabeth's advice but I didn't know how to *not* fight it. The pull on my magic was like a needle driven into the most fragile part of me, siphoning something too valuable to give up. I exhaled a steady breath between sentences, drawing too-hot air back into my lungs, the taste that coated my mouth enough to make me retch. I kept reading, had no choice *but* to keep reading. I'd begun, and if I stopped now, the demons would be upon us. There were too many of them.

It was stupid to call every demon in the country here and think I could hold them, stupid to—

I gasped when a cool rush of shadows moved over my skin, the sharp tug on my power easier to bear. I gave Rus a quick look of gratitude as I read, my heart full. I wasn't alone. It wasn't my power alone that would fuel this incantation. I had a circle, friends, family, allies. We could do this.

We *had* to do this, because hot breath hit my face as a bear-like demon drew close. Bonnie flew like a blur through the air to drive it back a hair's breadth away from me. My voice wavered, but I kept reading. I was halfway through now, and power rushed in from my left—embers and flickering fire, similar to mine but slow-burning where mine was a rapid charge of flames. Elsabeth. The pressure on my power lessened slightly, but it rebuilt with every word I yelled, having to shout louder, fiercer over the growls and the chilling clicking of claws or fingernails too close to my ear. I tried not to flinch, ignoring the catch in my breath as I read a line to cut off the demons' access to their magic. I had to trust the others to defend us.

All at once, the temperature dropped, the scalding air around the demons plunging back to the park's normal heat. I shuddered at the contrast. It was working. I kept reading, trying not to let hope get the better of me as more magic flowed into my chest—blackened light and rich velvet and light that was cold and bright enough to burn. It rushed through me and into the park with every line I shouted, every word a brick walling off the demons from their power. I wasn't ripping it out of them, just locking it within themselves where they could never access it. And judging by the riot of fury pelting us with spittle and snarls and threats in a dozen different languages, they'd already begun to lose access.

"Keep going," Rus urged, squeezing my wrist when I faltered at the red-scaled body that came so close its wing grazed my shoulder. Bourne and Corbinian drove into it with a sword each, both demonic and originally Corbinian's.

If the previous lines had pulled at my power, the next passage sank hooks in and dragged it away from all of us. Grunts and sharp inhales met my ears. I wanted to clench my jaw at how much it hurt, at the sudden tiredness that drove into me, but I had to keep reading. I had to keep going.

I fixed my eyes on the page and read, even as blood splattered my hands, staining the codex, even as roars came so close they blew hair off my face and raked air down my wings, even as our allies fought them back with single-minded ruthlessness, even as Will said, "Holy shit, the council's here."

I didn't know if the councillors who'd arrived were on our side or against us, but with a park full of demons all fighting against the invocation I yelled, I couldn't afford to look away from the codex. I had to trust everyone else to protect the circle as more and more power flowed from our friends, our family, and out through me. Goosebumps moved to cover my whole body, instincts screaming at me to look up, that my throat would be slit, my wings torn apart, my horns snapped off, my face gouged apart.

"Keep going. They're weakening," Vala encouraged breathlessly.

My own voice became breathy but I kept shouting,

refusing to let the exhaustion that gathered in my bones slow me down when this was *working*. The demons' anger grew even louder, sharper, hotter.

The vellum page swam before my eyes but I squinted and forged on, not liking the way my voice lost its power or volume. But it was strong enough, and I only had four lines left.

"Karina," Rus said urgently, squeezing my wrist. More magic flowed through me and into the demons, but my lips were growing numb and I didn't know how to regain control. Three sentences left. I could do this.

"You need to slow down," Elsabeth cautioned.

"She's almost done," Vala disagreed.

"Shut up," Isaiah snapped. "Don't distract her."

The page wavered in and out of focus, but I'd read it enough times that I knew them even blurry. Two lines left. Almost there, almost done. It didn't matter that my face was cold, my hands numb where I gripped the codex. One line left. Exhaustion made me as heavy as iron, my bones leaden. My head swum, dizziness striking so quickly I couldn't avoid it.

Seven words left. I shut out every noise, every movement I glimpsed in the edge of my vision. Power swelled within me, a blend of all our magic, building to a devastating crescendo.

Five words. Four. I was too cold. My lips struggled to form shapes. Three words. I ran out of air, the park turning black at the edges. Bone-deep tiredness tugged on me. Two words left. Just two. Moving my lips took gargantuan effort but I knew the words. Even when my knees buckled, Rus and Elsabeth rushing to hold me up, I forced my tongue to spit the final words.

And then it was done.

Silence fell over the park, the demons rendered mute in shock. Or maybe the silence was inside my own head. I had the vague sense of Rus pulling me against his body, of warmth against the chilled expanse of my body, but my consciousness ripped away and then there was only darkness and cold.

TWENTY-THREE

And then there was blood, hot and sweet and life-giving, pouring down my throat like liquid strength. I sucked it down on instinct, gulping until it was all I could taste, until I could feel my fingers again, until my face tingled instead of cold turning me numb. Something warm sat on my lap, so heavy my legs were going numb, but that didn't matter as much as the blood that soared through me, soothing the exhaustion until I felt strong, easing my aches and pains until I healed. When the heavy lump on my lap began to purr, I realised it was Keith and drew away from the blood with a jagged inhale.

"Rus?" I breathed, knowing the specific taste of his blood, his scent, his presence at my side.

"It's over," he said quickly, making quick passes up and down my back with his hand. His lips brushed my ear. "There are other councillors here. They know Ursula and her husband were behind all this. As far as they know, they were the ones who brought all the demons here, and that's how it's going to stay. We told them you stripped the demons' power to make them less of a threat, and we aided you with the power for such advanced magic, but that's all they know."

My head swam a little but I nodded. Okay. They didn't need to know I'd risked the whole city by calling thousands of demons into a single park. Or that I'd helped Lorn in Battersea Park.

"I told them I gave you a covert mission to infiltrate Lorn's cabal," Rus went on quietly. "Everything you've done since Hell has, as far as they know, been sanctioned by a councillor."

"Covert mission," I echoed with a ghost of a smile. "You make me sound like a spy."

He drew back enough to kiss my brow. "You were."

"Hey, asshole, give her a minute," Ruby snapped not too far away. "She just woke up because the magic she channelled fixing *your* cock-up knocked her out. A few minutes is the least you owe her."

That was Ruby alright. A smile tugged at my lips. The exhaustion I'd felt reading from the codex had been replaced with vitality, but I was still tired in my soul.

"No, actually," Ruby went on, not letting the other person speak. "We were nearly the food or slaves of demons, so I don't think I will lower my voice. As far as I see it, I'm the only human here so that makes me the mortal representative and you *will* listen to me. That maniac came from your council, everything that happened today was your fault, and the only reason we're not in literal Hell right now is because my best friend is a kind, altruistic badass who genuinely cares about the world. You should be on your knees thanking her."

Rus chuckled, squeezing my hip, reluctant to let go as I tried to unseat Keith and climb to my feet.

"That's overkill, Ruby," I called, lifting my head and searching the park for my best friend. She stood a few paces away with her arms crossed over her chest, her chin cocked dangerously, and her eyes fixed on a werewolf a whole head taller than her and twice as wide. Isaiah hovered behind her, ready to intervene should she need backup, but the councillor sighed and stepped away with a shake of his head.

"Your friend is scary," Lazarus remarked, helping me up. Keith yowled in disapproval as he was dumped ungraciously to the grass. His purring cut off when he glared up at us, but he held my gaze a moment too long, searching.

"I'm alright," I promised, ignoring the scratchy quality of my voice. I bent to pluck him off the ground and cuddled him close to my chest, jumping at the sudden roar of his purr. Rus scratched a spot behind his ear, Keith's eyes squinting shut in response.

"Aw, look at you three," Ruby said, jogging over. "You make such a cute, weird family. The Shadow Bringer, a badass demon-fighting vampire, and the cat that eats people."

"I haven't eaten you so I don't see what you're complaining about," Keith remarked.

"And speaks. The cat that speaks." Ruby's eyes fixed on mine, wide and stunned.

"You get used to it," I told her, a smile tugging at my

mouth. "It's really over?" I asked her, trusting her to give it to me straight.

"Yup." She ignored Rus's warning glare to approach, pulling me—and Keith—into a tight hug. His purring shot even louder; Ruby had to raise her voice. "The Order Force are here tagging all the demons. They'll be registered and watched to make sure they don't murder anyone the regular way—without magic. Crisis averted, world saved. Good job, Karina."

"Uh. Thanks. I really wasn't trying to save London; I just wanted to feel safe again."

She shrugged, her eyes remarkably bright to say she'd just fought in a horrific battle with demons that oozed and slimed and chittered. "Two birds, one stone."

"What have you done?" a weak voice came from somewhere to our left, rising higher. "What have you done?"

I watched with wide eyes as the other robed figure, the man—Ursula's *husband* did Rus say?—was marched toward the exit, surrounded by guards.

"Heads up," Isaiah warned, the slight warmth of his expression icing over as a man strode over to us in red-edged black jacket and trousers, horns curling from the sides of his shaggy brown hair and his tanned face tight with irritation.

"This came for you," he grunted, thrusting an envelope at Lazarus and giving the rest of us a look down his nose. "For future reference, I'm not a fucking messenger."

Isaiah's expression flattened further. "Look at her like that again, and I'll melt those horns from your head."

Ruby rolled her eyes.

The horned man just sighed and turned away, muttering, "I don't get paid enough for this shit."

"He seems nice," I drawled, trying not to look at the patches of grass still smoking, life and greenery charred black. Trees had been ripped from the ground, the lake frothed with a black, viscous fluid that was far from normal, and the bridge had been snapped in half. I did this, by calling all of them here.

"He's a junior councillor who thinks the sun shines out of his backside," Isaiah replied with a frown. "Ignore literally everything that comes out of his mouth and every look he gives you. And stop feeling guilty. You prevented a dangerous coup on mortal parliament and saved us from exposure. Today's a good day."

I swallowed the knot in my throat and nodded. "Was anyone hurt?"

"Not badly enough that they can't heal," Rus told me, his hand finding my waist, the letter tucked away. "A week's rest and we'll be fine. As for the demons, you never have to worry about them ever again. They'll be relocated and monitored by the Order Force. It's really over, baby vamp."

I glanced away, emotion hitting me suddenly, my eyes stinging. "Did any of them get out of the park—"

"No one was hurt," Rus said firmly. "You don't need to worry, and there's nothing to stress or feel guilty about. Sai's right. Today's a good day."

I'd been on edge, in constant fight or flight mode for so long that I didn't know what to do now. It left me shaky and raw.

"What's in the letter?" Ruby asked, eyeing Rus with

something like a warning. I couldn't have said who'd win in a battle of wills between those two. Rus was stubborn but my friend didn't take no for an answer, ever.

"A response from Charis to a message I sent weeks ago. After today's events, it contains a full pardon."

My eyes shot to his, breathing suddenly difficult. "For what?"

"For everything," he replied softly. "Any crime listed in the database attached to your name has been erased." I really was going to cry. "You don't have to fear Order Force officers coming to arrest you in the night. You don't have to worry about being pulled in by the council or locked up or any of that."

I closed my eyes tight, tensing my mouth to stop the quiver in my bottom lip. Even with the demons under control, even with the city safe—me safe—I hadn't thought to hope for *this*. It really was over, all of it.

"Of course any future crimes you want to sneak out and commit will be attached to your record," Rus said with amusement. "But as far as past allegations, you're cleared."

He must have seen the expression on my face, or felt the tempest of emotion drawing me under, because he gave Ruby and Isaiah a pointed look and pulled me into his arms when they gave us a moment's privacy.

"What do I do now?" I asked in a small voice. "There's no Lorn to come after me, no Keaton, no officers, no councillors. So... what now?"

"Now," Rus said, thumb stroking circles on the base of my spine, "you live. You learn how to wield that remarkable power of yours. You put that incredible mind of yours to work on whatever cause or job calls to you." He kissed my head. "And you go home, and spend time with your mum."

"But my thirst—"

"Is under control. You've mastered it Karina. When was the last time you were out of control around mortals? You just spoke to Ruby, a human, and never once even thought about drinking from her."

Now he mentioned it my fangs ached and my throat went dry with thirst, but... he was right. "I can go back?"

His smile was devastatingly soft. "You can go home, Karina."

I didn't know how I'd ever look Mum in the eye and tell her what happened to Jubilee. I didn't know if I could ever tell her, ever speak about it, but I wanted to see her with a fierceness that made my chest hurt. But that house wasn't home anymore. I'd changed too much, been through too much, to fit where I used to.

"Let's go see my mum," I said, glancing at Keith when he wriggled in my arms. "And then let's go home. To *our* home."

And whatever came after, I'd face it the same way I'd faced everything since that night in the library—with courage, panic, magic, and books. Lots and lots of books.

THANK you so much for reading Karina's series! I hope you enjoyed the conclusion to the Shadow Order: Vampire series.

There will be more books in this world, beginning

with Vala's series, Shadow Order: Demon! The series will begin early 2026, and I can't wait to share all her snark and magic with you. If you'd like an alert when it's available, you can follow me on Amazon or join my newsletter.

While you wait, try the Coven of Magic series for witches, elves, magic, and small town fantasy vibes with slow burn romance.

If you loved this book, I would hugely appreciate a rating or review - both help readers decide whether to read a book, especially from a new-to-them author.

I'll see you in the next book!

Kristin x

FREE URBAN FANTASY ADVENTURE!

Meet Grace Kincaid, fairy tale huntress.

Hunting a fairy tale was never Grace's plan, but when Bluebeard kidnaps her sister, Grace sets out to find him, kill him, and rescue Clara.

Several things have the nerve to get in her way: Bluebeard's silken compulsion magic, her own recklessness, and Eden Latimer, an anti-tale officer hell bent on saving Grace's life.

But Grace won't let anything come between her and her sister's safety. Even if she has to enter Bluebeard's dollhouse and rescue her herself.

JOIN MY MAILING LIST FOR YOUR FREE STORY

SIGNED KRISTIN KOVA BOOKS!

You can find all my available print copies in my online book store, **and all signed orders come with a dedication from yours truly.**

START READING COVEN OF MAGIC

The word naughty was carved deep into the girl's cheek, bone-white skin peeling back to expose muscle and bone. Discarded in the sand beside her—and almost worse than the gruesome cut—was the girl's wand. It was slim and ebony and snapped into two pieces, with jagged splinters on the ends.

As soon as Joy Mackenzie registered what she was seeing—the wand, the blood, and the fact that the girl was actually a corpse—she skittered away with a cry, tripping over her boots and falling onto her ass on the grassy sand dune. Bile rose into her throat as she looked and looked at the girl, unable to tear her eyes away even as her stomach wrenched against her breakfast.

When she spotted the shape from across the beach, Joy presumed it was Old Josie, passed out on the beach again after one too many sherries. Not a dead girl with half her face carved off.

"Oh, god..."

Joy twisted aside as her stomach cramped, bile

scorching her throat as she was violently sick into the sand.

Wiping her mouth on the sleeve of her coat and gagging as grains of sand clung to her lips, Joy looked across the beach to the blocky yellow hut of the nature reserve where she worked. It was hard sometimes to separate the structure from the sand dunes that cradled it, but a fat beam of sunlight caught the windows as Joy turned towards the building, like a divine figure sensed her desperation and sent help. But Joy was opening up the reserve today, and it was too early for even the most dedicated beach joggers to be out. There was nobody to help Joy, no one to tell her what to do about the girl rotting in the sand before her.

Clumsy, her eyes fixed on that yellow hut so they didn't return to the dead girl, Joy climbed to her feet, her stomach roiling again as her boots slipped on the sand. What she really wanted was to go home and bolt all her locks. But she couldn't leave the girl, the ... body, here. It wasn't right, and Joy had always tried to do the right thing, even if it was difficult and she would probably be sick again.

On her feet, she fumbled in her pocket for her phone and took deep breaths to settle her stomach as she scrolled through her contacts to a number she hadn't used in years.

There hadn't been a murder in this town for as long as Joy had been alive. Back in the seventies, people were killed scarily often, usually the victims of inter-species fights, fae gang wars, or personal grudges—but then Clover Pride, one of the most powerful elves in the North, decreed herself Agedale's law enforcement, later joined by her husband, Bo. Clover had somehow earned respect from every species that lived in town, and, with her husband, they were as close as the community came to patrol, investigators, enforcers, and problem solvers all rolled into one.

But Clover Pride died years ago—Joy still remembered the shock and standstill all across Agedale as the news spread—and Bo had been injured on the job, forced to retire a year ago. Now, the closest they came to law enforcement was Head Witch Paulina, the leader of Agedale's only recognised coven, but she cared less about justice than having her every command followed. She was more a politician than a police officer. Joy had known the break-ins would start again, the inter-species spats, but … murder?

With the word cut into the baby-faced teenager's cheek, so fresh and violent in Joy's mind even as she faced away, there was no chance this was an accident.

Joy pulled the collar of her coat—a fluffy, oversized grey thing—further up her neck and ducked against the salty wind as she held her phone to her ear.

"Hi, sorry, it's Joy—Joy Mackenzie. I didn't know who else I should call. I've found a … there's a girl on the beach near my work, the reserve on the western edge, the yellow one with the solar panels on the roof, and there's—"

"Joy," said Bo Pride calmly. "Breathe. What do you mean there's a girl?"

"She's dead. I mean—I didn't check, I really should have, but I thought it was Josie at first, so I didn't even think to check her pulse, but there's …" Joy took a breath, but it was little more than a scrape of air. How did she explain the word carved into the girl's cheek? Or the gore of half her face hanging off? "I think she's been murdered."

CONTINUE JOY'S story in Coven of Magic, which is out now!

ABOUT KRISTIN KOVA

Kristin Kova is an urban fantasy author from the UK. She writes about relatable women who kick ass, dangerous fictional men, and magic-packed stories full of heart and action with a side of sizzling steam.

All four books in her first series, The Shadow Order: Vampire, are out now, and you can pick up two urban fantasy stories for free by joining her newsletter.

FIND THESE OTHER BOOKS BY KRISTIN KOVA

The Shadow Order: Vampire

(*complete series*)

Vampire Librarian

Vampire Shadow

Vampire Sight

Vampire Legion

The Shadow Order: Demon

Demon Night - coming soon!

Coven of Magic series

FREE: Coven Trial

Coven of Magic

Coven of Shadows

Coven of Storms - Winter 2025!

Huntress of Evil - free novella!

www.ingramcontent.com/pod-product-compliance
Lightning Source LLC
Chambersburg PA
CBHW032143170626
46808CB00006B/2353